SPANISH NIGHTS

A JINN'S SEDUCTION BOOK 1

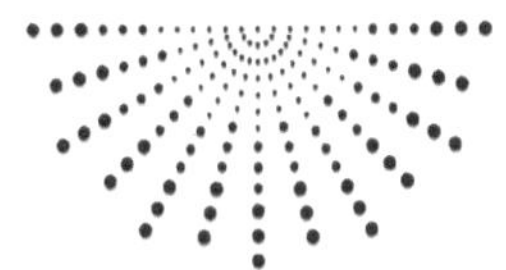

VALERIE TWOMBLY

SPANISH NIGHTS

A JINN'S SEDUCTION

By
Valerie Twombly

Spanish Nights

DEDICATION

This book is dedicated to my street team, Valerie's Fang Gang. You gals rock and I love you all!

ACKNOWLEDGMENTS

Special Thanks:
Ana P Martinez, for helping with my Spanish
Patricia Cookson, for coming up with the moonstone amulet
Robin Malone, for coming up with the chant

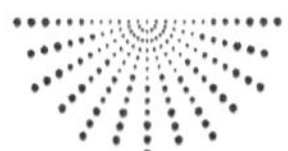

House of Unaria, 1100 AD.

"You're a fool," Cyndel screeched.

Armand's skin crawled.

"I believe it is you who are the fool. Why would you want me to marry you when I don't love you?" The entire conversation perplexed him. He wasn't ready to contemplate marriage and especially to the crazed genie who stood before him. Yet deep down, he knew the real reason. She had seduced him. Promised him nights of passion with no commitment. She was much older and he had only been a fledgling at the time. Naive and powerless to walk away, the woman had sunk her talons deep into him and all he could think of was fucking her. Now that he was a full Jinn, and about to gain his own house to rule, she had changed the game plan. However, there was one thing she hadn't counted on. Armand was done being used and ready to walk away.

Cyndel glided closer and ran a sharp red nail down his bare chest. His flesh pimpled and his shaft stiffened. The woman knew his weakness and intended to play him for a fool. He stifled a laugh. It was she who was foolish if she thought fucking him would put a ring on her finger. No, he'd gladly scratch her itch, but that was all. He was willing to give his cock and nothing more. She straddled his lap and ground her hot sheath into his groin.

"I can make you change your mind." She nibbled his earlobe, her fingers wrapping around his dark locks and pulling hard. "Besides, you will grow to love me. It doesn't have to be on our wedding day."

He groaned under her administrations. The woman was breathtaking, her body sweet perfection and impossible to resist. He caressed the soft underside of her breast and let his fingers blaze a trail to her nipple, where he pinched the sensitive bud and gave a slight twist. She tipped her head back. Her raven hair nearly touched the floor and a moan escaped her lips. Armand couldn't help but smile. He also knew how to strum her body and make her beg for more.

"I can hear your thoughts, Armand." She met his gaze. Her violet eyes swirled with desire. "Do not overestimate your talent."

He pinned her to the stone floor, not caring if the cold seeped through her body or the rocks ripped it to shreds. Cyndel had used him for the last time and now it was his turn. She gyrated beneath him and he latched on to a nipple. Sucking it into his mouth, he scraped his teeth over the distended point while he pressed his erection between her thighs.

"Take me, Armand."

He raised his head so he could look upon her beauty. She would make a good wife if not for her greed, and the fact she would never be faithful. He couldn't count how many times she'd cheated on him in the years they'd been together. At first he'd been hurt. As he grew older and wiser, he realized what she really wanted was his power, and he simply couldn't conjure any feelings for her other than the fire in his groin. He needed more from the woman who would become his queen. He needed love.

"You're a dirty whore, Cyndel."

"Stop talking and give me your cock."

He pushed the flimsy skirt past her waist then pulled his silk trousers down until his erection sprang free. In one fluid motion, he was buried deep. Her hot sheath wrapped around him and squeezed. Their magic swirled, lifting them off the floor and into an exotic air dance. He pulled back then thrust. Her nails dug into his back laying the flesh open, but he felt no pain as the wounds healed instantaneously. He brought her closer until her breasts pressed against his chest. They rocked in unison, caring for nothing else but the moment. He fisted a handful of black hair. Jerking her head back, he suckled the tender spot between her neck and shoulder. He nipped, moved upward until his lips were at her ear.

"Milk me you filthy bitch," he growled.

She screamed. Her body shuddered in orgasm and her muscles clamped tight. Armand smiled, his dirty talk always sent her over the edge. Her pleasure was easy and predictable.

Cyndel flipped them in mid-air putting him beneath her. Her skirts flowed around him obstructing his view, so he grabbed the hem and ripped. The sight of his shaft, slick with her desire, made him harder. She rode him like a stallion. Fast and hard. The bitch needed to come at least three times before she'd be sated. Armand moved his thumb to cover her nub and rubbed in a circular motion.

She exploded and he had to bite back his own release. If he jilted her, she would nag him to the ends of the universe. He spun then brought them back to the floor and pressed her again the glass window. Placing his hands under her ass, he lifted her feet off the ground and pushed his rigid flesh between her swollen lips. He wondered if her guards were getting an eye full.

"You like being on display? Perhaps the guards will come and fuck you like a dog when I've finished," Armand growled. He knew the thought of being seduced by several of the armed men outside would have her screaming in ecstasy. Not that she hadn't already used every guard in her army. It was her dirty little secret, but the men liked to talk. Hell, who wouldn't brag at having a go with Cyndel? The trick was to keep the whispers from reaching her. Piss her off and she could hold a grudge for centuries. The thought caused him to shudder. He met her violet gaze. "Come for me, Cyn."

Each thrust of his hips grew faster. She needed to hurry before he spilled his seed.

Cyndel dug her heels into Armand's behind as the third orgasm racked her body. With a final thrust he reached his own release. As his breathing returned to normal, he pulled free and set her on her feet. The genie smoothed the torn fabric of her skirt.

"As always that was wonderful, but we need to get down to business." The corner of her lips turned up into a devilish grin.

Armand grabbed his pants and pulled them on. "What business would that be?"

"Our wedding arrangements, of course."

He sighed. Cyndel wasn't going to relent. She'd been pushing to bring their houses together. With her father as ruler of the House of Unaria and Armand's own father king of Reviana, merging the two families would bring great wealth and power. He had worried for a time that even his father would side with the crazy genie, but he had told his son it was his choice alone who he married and when. Armand couldn't help the pride that filled his chest when he thought of his family.

His father, Efrain, a powerful Jinn had ruled the house of Reviana for thousands of years. Armand being the eldest prince stood next in line. Next week, on his five-hundredth birthday he would be given his father's house to rule. It was one of the reasons Cyndel was so adamant on marriage.

Next came his brother Crone, followed by the baby Lazaro.

"Cyn. I don't know how to make it more clear to you." He stepped closer and cupped her chin, tipping her head up to meet his gaze. "Sex with you is great, but that's all it is. I don't love you and you can't force me to. It's time we end this."

Her violet eyes swirled with flecks of black. Anger rose off her and slithered across his skin leaving bumps in its wake.

"I suggest you rethink your refusal, Armand."

He released her chin and stepped back. "You can not make me love you and idle threats do not frighten me." He fisted his hands at his side. Ready for whatever she would throw at him.

Cyndel smiled. "As you wish then." She tipped her head then vanished.

Armand released his stance. Cyndel was pissed, but she'd get over it. He quickly finished dressing and headed for the door to make a hasty exit before she decided to return. He wasn't ready to deal with her foul mood. He flung open the heavy oak panel and black mist trailed around his waist, sucking him into a vortex.

ARMAND'S CHEST CONSTRICTED, and hard as he tried, he couldn't bring air into his lungs. His pulse pounded in his temples as darkness surrounded him. He struggled to stay conscious. A loud snap resonated through his body.

A rift had opened.

He plummeted through space and slammed onto some jagged rocks. He grunted and tried to relax his muscles as he continued to roll over the rough terrain. Coming to rest, he realized his head throbbed and something warm ran down the back of his neck. The winds whipped up and tossed bits of ice, like millions of tiny razors, at his flesh.

He winced through the pain. *What have you done to me, Cyndel?*

Dressed in thin silk pants and no shirt, his teeth chattered from the biting cold that wrapped around him. He listened through the howling in his ears but could detect no other sounds of life. Armand tried to keep his eyes open, but his lids weighted down and before long they slammed shut.

The distant sound of a crackling fire and the scent of oak reached through the fog in Armand's head. He forced his eyes open and tried to focus on the fireplace across the room. Beneath him lie a soft bed and his body was covered with a down quilt. His mind told him to stay settled into the warmth, but the warrior in him said to get up. First, he wiggled his toes and fingers. Then he tested his arms and legs. Everything seemed to be in working order. Next, he lifted his head and noted the ache that had resided there earlier was gone. He sat up, letting the quilt fall to his lap, and took in the surroundings. In a large hearth on one side of the room, a roaring fire blazed that contained a cast iron pot with steam curling up toward the chimney.

Next to him were two wooden chairs and in one sat his brother.

"Glad to see you have finally awakened." Crone leaned back, arms folded over his broad chest and one brow cocked upward. The man looked like his patience had reached its limit.

"Where the hell am I?" Armand tossed the quilt aside and set his feet to the cool wooden floor. Standing, he strode to the warmth of the fire not caring he was naked.

"Well, it would seem you pissed of Cyndel and she has cursed you."

Armand whipped around and faced his brother. "Curse?"

Crone examined his nails. "Yes, brother, curse. You do remember what that is?"

Armand crossed his arms. "Yes, I fucking remember. What kind of curse?"

Crone looked up and rolled his eyes. "For the love of god, put some damn clothes on." He waved to the foot of the bed. "I'm really not in the mood to stare at your goods."

Armand mumbled under his breath and grabbed the black silk pants. He shoved his legs in and pulled them up to settle on his hips. "Better? Now tell me what you know."

Crone stood and produced a crystal decanter of amber liquid and two glasses. He filled each halfway then handed one to Armand. "Cyndel has sent you to earth." He sipped. "To be exact, we are sitting right below our home. She has stripped you of all your power." His brother stepped in front of him; sympathy swirled in his eyes. "With the exception of your immortality and ability to heal ... you are human."

Armand growled and threw the crystal against the floor. Shards of glass mixed with a pool of amber liquid. "I assume father is working on the situation?" His chest heaved. Certainly Efrain would have this fixed and he would soon be back home.

"Of course he is, but Cyndel has gone into hiding and no one can locate her. Her family claims they have no idea where she is." Crone shrugged. "I spoke to her briefly before she vanished. It was apparent while she was severely pissed, she didn't want your death. I was allowed to come attend to your needs and see you settled here on earth. However, I can only stay for twenty-four hours before I'm ripped away. Then I can visit once every six months. You will have to make do on your own."

Armand set his jaw. "I don't suppose the bitch told you how to break this curse?"

"Afraid not."

Armand turned away from his brother. He didn't want the younger Jinn to see his panic. Instead, he focused on the flames and watched them consume the log like a starved hound. He tried to reach out and grasp the fire with his power, roll it in his palm and call to its strength, but it no longer recognized him as its master. It ignored him like an obstinate child.

The pain cut through him like a hot blade. Everything he knew was gone: his way of life, his family and his very being. However, he was Jinn and prince of the House of Reviana. He would not allow himself to indulge in self-pity.

He pulled back his shoulders and turned to face Crone. "Search every corner of the universe if you must, but find a way to break this curse."

Crone tipped his head. "You know I will never stop." He faded away leaving Armand alone.

He clenched his fists. "Cyndel, you should have killed me because if I ever break this spell, I will destroy you."

CHAPTER ONE

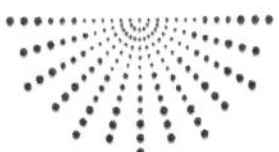

Makayla stared at the blinking curser on her laptop, it mocked her and reminded her of how useless her life had become. Many years ago, she'd been a New York Times best selling author and at the top of her game, but she hadn't written a word in two years. She tried. God knew she'd tried everyday. Perched in her chair, she'd open her laptop and watch the page go from white to fuzzy gray. After a couple of hours, she'd give up and walk away in frustration. The truth was it scared her shitless. If she didn't produce something soon, both her agent and publisher were going to drop her like yesterdays news.

"Maybe you need to take a vacation. Some place exotic?"

She snorted and looked over the top of her computer at Nikki. The two had been best friends since high school, but Nikki had followed a modeling career while Makayla worked hard to get her first novel published. Fatal Desire had been a dark romance between a dragon shifter and his demon mate. She'd been fortunate to find an agent who'd sold her manuscript to a large New York publisher. The book had been an instant success and put her on the bestseller lists. Three books followed in the series along with a marriage to a man she had considered her soul mate.

That was four years ago.

A year after they vowed to love and honor each other, she caught Eric sleeping with another woman. She'd been devastated.

Nikki closed the magazine she'd been flipping through and tossed it on the glass coffee table. She slipped in behind Makayla and rubbed her shoulders. "A blank screen." Nikki sighed. "I have a friend who owns a home in a small village in Spain. It's remote and beautiful. The people are wonderful. Let me call him and see if it's available."

Makayla pulled the lid closed on her laptop knowing there would be no words written today. Hell, she hadn't written since the divorce. The bastard had broken her heart and taken her muse. "I don't know. A trip does sound wonderful but Spain? That's just crazy."

Nikki spun the chair so they faced each other. "Seriously? Kayla, you need to see this place. You'll fall in love, and the best part is it's rent-free. You only need to get there."

She chewed her lip. It was tempting, but she'd never left the country before unless she counted Canada.

"I can hear your brain rattling. Stop looking for an excuse."

"I don't need an excuse. Spain is a long way away from home and I don't know anyone there." If she were honest with herself, it both scared her and excited her at the same time.

Nikki rolled her eyes. "Oh for god sakes, Kayla, take a risk. You took one a long time ago, remember? You wrote your first story and sent it off to that list of agents. Remember all the rejections you got?" Nikki sighed. "You didn't give up. You went back out there with a new list and started over."

Sympathy pooled in her friends eyes.

"Take a risk again. Don't let that asshat ex of yours ruin your life. Take it back, sweetie, and have the last laugh."

Makayla's pulse raced. Her friend had a point. If she got away from here, maybe her mind would finally clear and she could write. She rubbed her hands together and tried to warm them. "You're coming with, right?"

Her friend shook her head. "I'd love to, but I have a big shoot coming up. Besides, maybe for once in your life you can be warm. The weather there is beautiful." Her bottom lip curled upward. "Who knows, you might meet a handsome Spaniard who will heat your bed and give it to you good."

Makayla rolled her eyes and shoved her friend out of the way. Standing, she headed toward the kitchen for a glass of wine to take the chill off. The doctors never figured out why her body stayed cold even in the heat of the summer. Great Nana had said she needed the fire to complete her. Kayla had never understood the old woman and her crazy tales. "I'm perfectly fine not having sex."

Nikki snorted. "No woman is fine not having sex for two years. It's just not natural." She followed her to the kitchen. "Besides, how can you write a steamy romance when you've forgotten how to fuck?"

She unscrewed the cap to the bottle of Moscato and filled her glass to the rim. Setting the bottle on the counter, she pushed it toward her friend. Nikki was like a sister to her. She'd stop in and stay for as long as she could between assignments and she'd been there when Makayla had to go to court for the divorce. Nikki had been her rock. She took a long sip of wine, letting the sweet taste coat her tongue. God, her friend was right though. She'd let Eric ruin her life, but could she pick up the pieces again?

"It's not that I don't want sex." She closed her eyes trying to remember what it felt like to be wanted and realized she had no idea. Eric certainly hadn't needed her. Did a man exist that could make her the center of his world or was she living in a fairy tale? "You're right. How can I write romance when I've forgotten what it's all about?" She opened her lids to find her friend staring at her, a twinkle in her green eyes.

"Then I can call?"

"Why not? I've got nothing to lose." Makayla raised her glass and the girls clinked the cheap crystal together. Maybe this would be the turning point she desperately needed.

AFTER A NINE-HOUR FLIGHT and four hours on a bus, Makayla was exhausted to put it mildly. As they reached the top of the mountains and headed into a small valley, the village came into view. Her excitement grew. She'd never left the country before and truth be told, Spain had always been at the top of her wish list. She was lucky to have such a good friend in Nikki; even more so that Nikki had friends in high places. She would have never been able to afford to rent a villa in this sleepy, little town.

As she gazed through the dirty window, she noted how the homes were sprawled out from the town square and grew bigger in size as they reached the outskirts. It was obvious the people with money either lived or vacationed here.

The sun was low in the sky by the time they pulled into the local service station that doubled as the bus station. Darkness would be upon them soon. Kayla departed the bus and searched for the people designated to take her to the villa where she'd be staying.

A young man, who appeared to be in his teens, stood with a sign in his hand that read: Makayla. She approached. "Hello, do you speak English?"

The boy's face lit up. "Oh yes, *senorita*. Are you Makayla?"

She giggled. "I am. I just need to get my bags and then we can go. So what's your name?"

"Lucas, and I will help you with your cases."

She smiled. "Your English is very good. Oh look, they're unloading now."

The pair walked back to the bus and grabbed the two suitcases she'd brought. "Okay, lead the way."

Lucas waived his hands in the air. "No. No. Let me carry those for you."

"Okay," she laughed and followed him to a bright yellow Volkswagen Beetle where he popped open the trunk and shoved her bags inside.

With a slam of the lid, he smiled. "Get in and I'll drive you to your villa."

She folded herself into the passenger seat and in no time they were buzzing along a winding street dotted with white stucco villas. After ten minutes, he pulled in front of a small one-story building surrounding by a wrought iron fence.

"This one is yours. The Nolan home." He jumped out of the car and pulled her bags from the trunk. With one in each hand, he rolled them up the walk and unlocked the door.

Makayla followed him inside, pulled some cash from her purse and stuffed it into his hand. "Thank you very much."

He nodded and gave her a wide smile. *"Gracias, señorita."* Then ran back to his car.

She shut the door and flipped on the wall switch. The living room and kitchen were one big room covered in terra cotta tile. A brown suede sofa sat facing a large screen TV. The kitchen, with its brightly painted cabinets lent a perfect contrast.

She stifled a yawn, grabbed her bags and headed to find the bedroom. Jet lag had set in and she desperately needed sleep. Too tired to unpack, she climbed into bed and fell asleep to the scent of Jasmine carried in by the breeze.

Morning brought sunlight filtering through the vanilla colored sheers. She stretched and threw off the covers. Looking across the room, she remembered she hadn't even unpacked yet so she rolled out of bed and made her way down the short hall to where her luggage still stood by the front door. Pulling the bags behind her, she stopped mid-way to the bedroom.

"Oh, coffee." She eyed the machine sitting on the counter and prayed there was something to put in it.

After a quick look in the refrigerator, she found the coffee and set the pot to brew while she headed for the shower.

Thirty glorious minutes later she was clean and sipping a steaming cup of caffeine in the tiny courtyard to the rear of her villa. Colorful garments floated in the breeze on a clothesline behind her and were framed by white-capped mountains. The scene was surreal. Next on the list, a walk around the neighborhood and then she'd unpack.

CHAPTER TWO

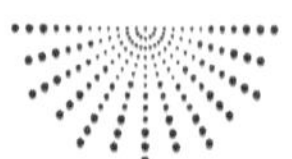

$\mathcal{A}$rmand stared out the window and looked down the hillside at the village. His village. A place that had first been his purgatory was now his home. As if he'd had a choice. Cyndel had condemned him to the Pyrenees Mountains of Spain but his real home was high above the mists.

Stripped of his Jinn magic and unable to leave the mountain range, he had built a life here as best he could. A modest cabin had turned into a tiny village and now it was a small town with all the modern-day conveniences. Because he'd retained his immortality, he had to be resourceful so the people here wouldn't become suspicious. They believed his forefathers were the original founders and builders of their small community. That meant he had to make an excuse to leave for several years then venture into a cave his brother, Crone, had carved out for him with his magic. There he lived until the locals grew older, and he would come back stating he was a relative of the deceased and start his life over again.

It was a lonely existence to say the least, one he hated and had been his hell for several hundred years. No matter what his family had tried, they had been unable to break the curse, but Armand refused to give up hope. There had to be a way to return him to his former life, though he wasn't sure he even remembered how to be a Jinn. Armand hadn't felt his Jinn stir since he'd been imprisoned here. Often the heat was so unbearable he would lie in a tub of ice just to cool down. Being unable to release his power or shift to smoke was like keeping an animal in a cage. He was slowly suffocating.

After a few hundred years, Armand had finally grown accustomed to living as a human and had come to love the people of his community. They relied on him and he threw himself into looking after their needs. There wasn't a building in this town he hadn't assisted with either financially or physically. Thanks to Crone, who brought him gold and jewels during his visits, he had at least been able to live comfortably.

He turned from the window and strode to the front door, stopping to look at the pictures of his family. Crone had been kind enough to take the photos and frame them, then hang them as a gift. Efrain, his father, looked every bit a king. His jet-black hair was kept short, but his chiseled face showed a little wear. Armand wondered if he had caused his father's stress and it ate at him. His entire family had tried to reason with Cyndel and except for the fear of Armand never being released from his curse, his brothers would have killed her.

Next was Crone, the only family member allowed to visit, and he was grateful for that. The others had tried, but the curse Cyndel had used kept his loved ones away. For some reason however, Cyndel had allowed Crone to come once every six months. It was the only thing that kept him sane.

Lazaro was the baby. Only a child when Armand had been cast out, the photo now showed a grown man, and it pained him he had missed his little brother growing up.

He fisted his palms. Anger bubbled up that Cyndel had caused him so much anguish because of her greed. He'd actually considered years ago giving in and marrying her, but Crone had assured him the family would get through the nightmare. His father wanted him to hold onto his beliefs.

He stared at Lazaro's picture. He would have already reached his immortality: the time when he stopped aging and his looks froze. His baby brother had always held a special place in his heart. He looked so much like their mother who had died in childbirth. It was the only time a female was vulnerable. He remembered his father's devastation. His parents had loved each other with every fiber of their souls. It was a love Armand had hoped one day to have and the reason why he refused to marry Cyndel. Now he kept his heart locked behind a frozen block. He couldn't love a mortal then watch her grow old and die. And what of their children? He could never bear to watch his offspring pass before him. Instead he acted the playboy, satisfied his needs then moved on, always painfully aware of the many broken hearts he left in his wake. It was better that way.

Armand scooped up the bouquet of violet orchids he'd picked from the garden earlier and walked out the door. The late morning sun had already turned the air to a pleasant seventy degrees so he decided to walk. Following the brick path, he took a sharp right and headed down the hill. His mission today was to greet a visitor staying at the Nolan home. Armand had started the tradition of welcoming guests when the first settler had asked to build here. The Elders passed on to their children the stories of Armand's ancestors, how they always took time from their day to greet a lonely stranger, even housed and fed those passing through. Little did they know it was Armand himself. It was the only thing that gave him purpose. This town, these people. They belonged to him and he would always make sure they were cared for.

After several minutes, he found himself in front of the Nolan home knocking on the heavy wooden door. A scurry of footsteps met his sensitive ears before the door opened.

He took a step back. The most exotic vision filled the void. The woman was stunning. Wide, brown eyes filled with curiosity looked back at him. His gazed dropped to full red lips and the sudden urge to taste them had his mouth watering. He couldn't stop staring at her beauty. By all the gods, he'd lost his tongue and had forgotten why he was there.

❧

MAKAYLA HAD BEEN SURPRISED by a knock on her door, but even more so when she flung it open to find the most stunning pair of almond-shaped blue eyes she'd ever seen staring back at her. It took her only a moment to realize the pools of sapphire were attached to one gorgeous man.

She blinked.

Nope, still there and still just as breathtaking as before. Men like that only existed in … well, not where she lived anyway.

"Uh, can I help you?" God she hoped he spoke English. Nikki had assured her there wouldn't be any problems with language here. She didn't know a lick of Spanish. Wait … was he holding flowers? She blinked again.

"Good morning, *señorita.*" He tipped his head and it was then she really took notice. His hair, a warm brown, hung in messy waves to his collar. The sun glistened off it, catching the golden highlights that made her want to touch each curl and entwine it around her fingers.

"My name is Armand. I'm here to welcome you to our small community." He thrust the flowers in front of her. "For you."

She reached for the bouquet, fighting to keep her hand from trembling. His thick Spanish accent made her want to drool. *God, I need to stop staring.* "Thank you, these are beautiful." His fingers touched hers as she grabbed the flowers and sent fire straight to her sex. Her imagination began to whirl with all the things those hot digits could do to her. She swallowed hard and pushed the thoughts from her head. *Great Kayla, nothing like wanting to hit on the first man at your door.*

"It's also customary that I give you a tour of our town, but first would you join me for coffee?"

"Coffee?" Had he just said something about a tour? Wait, how did a Spaniard have blue eyes?

He flashed a smile. "Unless you prefer tea or another beverage. The local cafe has lots of items to choose from. They also make wonderful sweet rolls if you haven't yet eaten."

"Umm, do you make it a habit to bring flowers and offer breakfast to strangers?" Makayla had been warned the people here were friendly. Still, it was weird to a girl who originally came from

Chicago; she found it difficult to shove away years of always being wary.

His smile remained. "Actually, yes I do. It's something my family has done for decades. My forefathers started this village many years ago and it's become a tradition to always welcome our newcomers with hospitality."

Now she felt like a total ass, and her gut told her the guy was genuine. "I'm so sorry. Of course, I'd love coffee and I haven't had time to see the village yet. I might incorporate it into my next novel. I bet there's a ton of history here."

He tipped his head. "You're a writer?"

Makayla stepped back from the door and decided it wouldn't hurt to invite him in. "I am. Would you care to come in? If you don't mind waiting, I'll place these in some water and change, then we can go."

"Thank you and please, take your time."

He strode into the small entry as if he owned the place and she couldn't help but take a look at his backside. She stifled a moan. Just as she suspected, the behind was just as delicious as the front. She slipped past, trying not to touch him in the small confines of the vestibule.

"Please come in and have a seat. I'll only be a couple of minutes." She directed him to a chair in the living room then headed for the kitchen to find a vase. After procuring the glass from an open shelf, she spun around to find the sexy Spaniard standing directly behind her. Had he been any closer, their bodies would have greeted each other in a most intimate fashion.

She looked up into his beautiful eyes and swallowed. "Oh, goodness. You startled me."

"My apologies, *señorita*, but I don't believe you ever told me your name."

She set the vase in the sink and filled it with water then moved it to the counter. He occupied the confined space of the kitchen, not only with his large frame, but something else. His mere presence commanded attention. There was a kind of power that exuded from him, and it made her a bit edgy in a way hard to define. Sexual? The man dripped sexual energy, but there was more to it. Kayla shook it off to simply being in close confinement with a Spanish god.

"I don't know where my manners are today." She extended her hand. "Hi, I'm Makayla Farren, but my friends call me Kayla."

He grasped her hand and brought it to his lips, which he brushed across the top of her knuckles ever so gently. His eyes met hers and darkened. In that moment, she sensed something familiar about him. That was impossible. They'd never met before. She fought to slow her pulse and tried to ignore the sensation his kiss left on her skin.

"*Señorita*, I hope you'll allow me to call you Kayla. It's a most beautiful name." His deep voice wrapped around her and caressed, causing bumps to skip across her skin. At the moment, she'd allow him to call her anything.

Kayla smiled. "I'd best change so we can go."

He released her hand. She backed away, turned and headed directly to the master suite at the back of the house. Closing the door behind her, she leaned against it and tried to catch her breath. She looked down and noted her hands shook along with her knees. Her skin tingled like it had been kissed by the sun and for once in her life she was warm.

"Okay, Kayla, center yourself. You're about to spend the morning with the most handsome man you've ever laid eyes on." She hurried across the room and grabbed her cell phone from the nightstand. Scrolling to Nikki's number she sent a quick text of thanks to her friend with a promise to follow up later.

She moved back to the other side and grabbed a pair of shorts from the dresser. Slipping her leg through the opening, she couldn't help the visions of him still racing in her head. Eyes so blue, they reminded her of a tropical lagoon. Then there was his body. Good god almighty, what a body. If it looked that good in jeans and a polo shirt, she could only imagine what he might be like nude.

"Christ, I need to stop before I spontaneously combust." She snapped the shorts, pulled on a T-shirt and ran a brush over her hair. She checked her reflection in the mirror. "This will have to do. It's not like you're going on a date, Kayla."

3

CHAPTER THREE

$\mathcal{A}$rmand watched in amazement as the girl known as Kayla fled the room. He'd met many beautiful women in his time, but this one had managed to do something not even he could.

Stoke the embers that were his Jinn.

When their fingers had touched, he felt a stir but wrote it off to his imagination. However, when he'd brushed his lips across her hand there had been no doubt. The Jinn long buried deep within him tried to roar to life. Was it simply a coincidence? There seemed to be something magical about her, but he couldn't put his finger on it. He would, though. His fingers, his tongue. He vowed as he stood in her small kitchen that he would take her in every room of the house. He would fill the small villa with her screams of pleasure and she would beg him for more. If such brief contact did this, then he could only hope fucking her might break his curse. He leaned against the counter and watched for her return. Why though? What was special about her? He searched his memories for anything that might fill in the gaps, but he had nothing.

He inhaled. The scent of strawberries filtered through his senses, stirring his cock. He licked his lips and couldn't help but wonder if she would taste as sweet as his favorite fruit.

Within minutes, the seductive female returned dressed in a pair of shorts and a yellow tee. His gaze moved directly to her breasts, noting how the fabric clung to the rounded mounds and accented them. Did she realize her nipples poked through the thin material and begged him to suckle one into his mouth?

Doubtful.

"I hope I didn't keep you waiting too long," she asked, flashing a sexy smile. Good gods, the woman was testing his restraint. He needed to keep his cool and remind himself *he* was the seducer, not the other way around.

"Not at all. Shall wc?"

"Yes. I'm looking forward to a stroll." She walked toward the door, but he arrived before her to open it.

"Allow me."

"Thank you." Kayla crossed the threshold to the outside while he closed the door behind him and double-checked the lock. Crime wasn't common in his small community. On the rare occasion when outsiders had thought to take what didn't belong to them, he'd made sure they were dealt with swiftly. Still, he felt the need to keep this woman safe.

Once outside, he offered his arm. She hesitated, as if unsure, but quickly regained composer and wrapped her fingers around his bicep. Her touch was cool and he was surprised he hadn't noticed it before. It soothed him like a refreshing balm.

He escorted her down the brick walk and turned left. The cafe was only a block away. "We'll have coffee first. You can tell me more about yourself and why you decided to visit our village."

She smiled at him. "Deal, but only if you tell me more about your family. I find it interesting that your descendants are the founding fathers."

"I'd be happy to tell you all about my family."

They reached the door of the restaurant, and he opened it allowing her to enter first. "This way." He led her across the small diner to a booth by the window. He waited for her to be seated before taking his own across from her then watched while she unfolded the napkin and placed it in her lap. Every move she made fascinated him. "Are you hungry?"

"I wasn't until the smell of those cinnamon rolls hit me on the way in."

"You will not be disappointed. *Café con leche* as well?"

She smiled and nodded. "Yes, please." She tucked a strand of hair behind her ear and he resisted the temptation to reach out and help her. He imagined the dark mass would feel like the finest silk fisted in his hand as he took her from behind.

Armand snapped his fingers. "Maria."

The woman quickly crossed the small café and Armand gave his order. In less than two minutes, she was back placing the rolls and coffee on the table. Before she could walk away, he touched her arm.

"How is your mother?"

"Much better."

"Good. You will let me know if she needs anything?"

"*Si* and *Gracias.*"

Armand turned back to the delightful morsel across from him who was sipping her coffee. "Maria's mother had a terrible fall a month ago and broke her leg."

"Oh that's awful."

He reached for a napkin and laid it over his lap. "Yes. They have very little money so I took care of the medical expenses. Maria insisted on paying me back so I let her work here to repay the debt. I tried to talk her out of it, but her family is proud." He leaned across the table. "Don't tell, but I'm putting the money aside so she can go to college next fall."

She finished chewing her roll. "That's so kind of you."

He lifted his shoulders. "They are good people and she deserves to go to school." He shifted in his seat. "So. Earlier you mentioned you were an author? Tell me more. What do you write about?"

Her cheeks turned a rosy pink and she chewed her bottom lip. He nearly groaned out loud, wanting to kiss and nip at the plump perfection before his tongue slid into her mouth and tasted every inch. He was positive she'd taste of strawberries. Plump, juicy and ripe for the picking.

"I write romance. Well actually, it's called paranormal romance." She took another quick sip of her coffee.

"Ahh yes. Sex with vampires and other mythological creatures." How perfect that his little vixen would be a master creator of such love stories. How would she take the news that he was one of them? Well a half-ass one at the moment, as he had no magic to back him up, but one nonetheless. Not that he would tell her even if he could prove it. He wondered why it even crossed his mind. Still ... would she roll her eyes at him? For some reason, it pained him slightly that she might take him as a joke.

She gave him a sheepish smile. "Yeah, that would be the kind of stuff I write about. Well, I used to anyway." She cast her gaze into her lap. "I'm surprised you're familiar with it."

"You'd be surprised at the things I know. Why do you no longer write?" He made a mental note to Google her name when he got home. He had the urge to read every word she'd ever written.

Kayla lifted her gaze to meet his and straightened her back, but she still looked as if the weight of the world sat on her shoulders. "I've been unable to write a word since my divorce two years ago."

The sadness he detected in her voice bothered him. "I'm sorry to hear that. Divorce is never easy." He had no idea how to comfort her. What did he know of divorce other than what he'd witnessed during his time on earth?

She stared out the window as if looking at something distasteful. "I caught him cheating and when we divorced I found I couldn't write. I've tried, but it's gone." She turned back to flash her brown eyes at him. The pain he saw there made him want to find her ex and rip his heart out. "My friend suggested this place. She thought getting away would help. I really need to get my shit together before my publisher dumps me."

Armand slid his hand across the table and touched hers. He had to push down the inferno that threatened to erupt. His Jinn clawed and scratched to reach the surface. He wanted this woman, here and now.

"I think you will find our small community inspiring. I will do whatever I can to assist." *Soon little one, you will be mine.*

❀

KAYLA COULDN'T DECIDE if she wanted to jerk her hand back or entwine her fingers in his. The heat that came off him seared her, yet she craved more. And what exactly did he mean by his comment? Maybe she was reading too much into the situation. He was here to simply show her the sites not seduce her. Though the latter would definitely be a bonus. She had learned before coming to the small village that the Spanish people were not only friendly but also flirtatious, so she was sure Armand meant nothing by his gestures. If he had, would she welcome his advances? Even go so far as to sleep with him? If she left her body in charge, there was no doubt she would go to his bed willingly. However, her mind was still grappling with the idea. She worried she'd never be good enough.

"Kayla?"

She jerked back to reality at the sound of her name rolling off his tongue. "Oh I'm so sorry. You must think me rude." She was sure her face was ten shades of red. *God why can't I get my shit together?*

"Not at all. I understand how one's past can come back to haunt them. I only asked if you were ready to take a walk."

Was there a mischievous glint in his eyes? "Yes, I'm very much looking forward to learning about the culture here."

Armand stood and held his hand out to her. She accepted and scooted across the bench to stand. He tucked her hand under his arm as he escorted her to the door. "First, I'd like to take you to a small park. I think you'll find the view astounding."

"Sounds wonderful." Kayla enjoyed the hardness of his muscles under her fingers and the contrasting softness of his shirt. He was several inches taller than her so she had to look up to stare into those blue depths.

They strolled down the brick walk lined with merchants, stopping in front of a small shop where a gentleman sat at a table outside. He worked with tiny pieces of gold that he painstakingly fashioned into a filigree bracelet.

"That's beautiful," Kayla commented.

Armand translated to the shopkeeper who smiled at Kayla and nodded.

"He thanks you. His family have been jewelers here for generations. Father teaching son and passing the tradition down the line."

"I'm definitely coming back to do some shopping later."

Next door, under a vibrant orange canopy, a man stood in the front window painting a scene of majestic mountains. He waved to them and Armand waved back.

Kayla watched in amazement as each stroke of his brush brought new depth to the landscape.

Moving along they passed shops filled with baked goods, their sweet smell wafting into the street, and merchants whose windows displayed colorful, hand-embroidered skirts and blouses.

As they approached the west end of town, the street disappeared and she found herself on a narrow path that weaved between stone buildings. Iron balconies dotted the structures and a few even had laundry hanging out to dry. Tenants waved from above as they walked passed.

"Armand."

Armand stopped. "Pedro, old man." He pulled the older gentleman into an embrace. "How have you been?"

"Good, *amigo*. I see you are giving the grand tour of our beautiful village." The elderly man beamed with pride.

"Yes. Pedro, this is Makayla. She is here for a brief vacation."

Pedro showed a toothy grin and extended his hand. Kayla accepted and as was the custom he planted a kiss on her knuckles. "Has Armand told you how his forefathers arrived here and built the first cabin?"

Kayla shook her head. "No. He hasn't."

The old man tucked her hand under his and led her to a nearby bench where he sat her down and regaled her with stories. She learned Pedro's great-great-grandfather had come here and started the first general store. Everyone admired Armand and his family. They just wished his brother Crone would visit more often.

"We should be going, Kayla," Armand murmured.

She hadn't realized they'd been sitting there for over an hour, but she had so enjoyed learning more about the sexy Spaniard. "Yes, of course." She rose and turned to Pedro. "Thank you so much. I really enjoyed the stories. Maybe we can chat again?"

The old man's eyes sparkled. "It would be my pleasure. Stop by here anytime, *chica bella*." He flashed a smile then glanced at Armand. "You take good care of this one, *amigo*."

Armand tipped his head then led Kayla down the path.

"The people here seem to love you. You must be very proud of what your family has created," Kayla said.

"I am very proud and the people here ... well, they are like my family," he replied.

"Pedro said you have a brother?"

"I do. Crone only visits a couple of times a year. He is very busy."

She thought she detected sadness in his voice. Maybe the brothers didn't get along or perhaps he simply missed him.

"Do you have any other family?" She studied his reaction and noted how his body tensed. Maybe it wasn't a good topic of conversation.

"I do, but they all live far away from here."

His tone led her to believe a change of conversation was in order, but before she could think of anything else they rounded a corner. The path widened, changing to grass and all the buildings faded away. Armand led her into a thicket of trees where the strong scent of evergreen filled the air. God, it had been forever since she'd been able to take a deep breath and fill her lungs with fresh clean air.

"It smells so good." Then she noticed the clearing in front of them. "Oh my god!" She released Armand's arm and raced ahead.

"I did not lie when I said it was beautiful." He came up beside her, but she couldn't take her eyes off the view. In front of her lay a vast lake. Water shimmered like a mirror in the sun's reflection. As spectacular as it was, the majestic snow-capped mountains that rose from the waters edge on the other side and reached for the heavens stole her breath.

Kayla plopped down in the grass and stared. "I've never in my life seen anything so stunning. I cannot even begin to find the words to describe it."

Armand sat beside her. His heat warmed her. "It's one of my favorite places. I can sit here for hours and watch the world go by."

She tipped her head and looked at him out of the corner of her eye. Damn, his rugged looks fit perfect into the setting. Was it the way his messy waves fell into his eyes? Or maybe the facial hair she wanted to touch so badly. Would it be coarse or soft? She pulled her thoughts back and returned to admiring Mother Nature. "I can certainly understand why. I think I could sit here for hours as well."

"I have an idea if you're up for it."

"What's that?"

"I know of a secluded spot that's great for swimming. We could go there tomorrow and I'll bring a picnic lunch."

She tore her gaze away from the view to look at him once again. Spending another day with this gorgeous man, alone, was worth saying yes. But to see him half dressed? To catch a glimpse of the muscle lurking beneath his shirt could bring back her muse. Besides, she enjoyed his company and wanted to learn more about the Spaniard.

"I think that sounds like a wonderful idea."

CHAPTER FOUR

Kayla leaned her forehead against the cool tile of the shower while the hot water sluiced down her back. She'd had a fitful night of sleep thanks to the sexy Spaniard. He'd had the audacity to show up in her dreams and make sexual advances, leaving her with a painful throb between her legs that she simply refused to address herself.

She was sick of 'taking care of business' as her friend Nikki put it. It only took one drop-dead gorgeous, Spanish-speaking man to make her realize what she'd been missing the past two years. Nikki had been right, she needed to get laid and the sooner the better.

With a new plan in mind, she exited the shower and toweled dry. Originally, she'd been going to wear her one-piece suit but change of plans. She decided on a bikini. Tossing the towel wrapped around her body into a laundry basket, she grabbed the suit bottom and pulled it up to settle low on her hips. Next came the top. She did a spin in front of the full-length mirror and gave a nod of approval. Kayla wasn't the type of woman who thought herself beautiful, though Nikki had always said she too could have been a model. Today, staring at her reflection in the ruby red suit did something for her ego. She'd always taken care of her body and had the curves to prove it. Armand wouldn't know what hit him.

Kayla topped off her ensemble with shorts and a tee then slipped on a pair of flip-flops. She glanced at the clock. Armand would be here in twenty minutes to pick her up. He'd assured her he would take care of everything. She only needed to dress for the occasion.

With nothing to do but wait, she sat on the couch and watched the clock tick. Bad move. Her nerves were beginning to get the better of her. *Maybe I should change. I mean what the hell am I thinking trying to seduce him? What if he turns me down?* She was being silly. If her intention was to get laid and she would only be in Spain for a few months, why not live it up? It wasn't like she was planning on marrying the man, and he'd be crazy to turn her down. Her intuition told her he was already interested.

She didn't have time to change her mind or her clothes before a knock came. Swallowing down her fear, she pulled up her courage before she flung open the door. Armand flashed a smile that would seduce her grandmother. Seeing him dressed in cut-offs and a white tee that hugged every muscle, she lost her voice.

"Are you ready?" His smooth accent caressed her. She could listen to him talk for hours and never grow tired of it. Matter of fact, she'd feel foolish admitting he made her wet between the thighs with every word he spoke. God, her mind briefly went back to her dreams of him telling her all the naughty things he was going to do to her. Some in Spanish and some in heavy accented English. She'd had no idea what he'd said, but it had been fun anyway.

Shit.

"Yes. Are you sure I don't need to bring anything?"

"No, I have towels and a picnic lunch all ready for us." He held out his hand. "Shall we?"

She slipped her hand into his and like before he tucked it under his arm. This time however, she gave his bicep a slight squeeze as they walked along the brick path and headed toward the park. Kayla couldn't help noticing again how his touch cocooned her in warmth.

Once more she dug for Nana's words. *Something about meeting a man whose fire ...* Damn, she couldn't remember.

Within minutes, they arrived at the lake's marina and he escorted her down a wooden dock to a boat. Kayla stopped mid-stride. For some reason, she'd expected a small craft. Instead, she found a cruiser with a cabin, and she couldn't help wondering if there were sleeping quarters below.

"Wait here and I'll help you."

Armand stepped aboard the vessel, grabbed her by the waist and picked her up. He slid her down the front of his hard muscles in the most intimate manner. Her nipples puckered and moisture flooded her apex before her feet hit the deck. If she questioned her earlier intentions of wanting this man to devour her, she didn't after the surge of arousal he stirred within her. Her body was on fire. Never had she experienced such intense heat.

"Ah, thanks." How she had managed to get the words out without stammering surprised her.

She followed Armand to the helm and took a seat. He pulled the rope free of the dock then slowly maneuvered the boat to open water. Once past the confines of the marina, he throttled up and they moved along at a nice clip. Kayla enjoyed the wind blowing across her skin. For once, she tried to cool herself rather then the other way around.

The view was even more breathtaking from the boat than it had been on land. White tufts in a blue sky floated by and majestic mountains reflected in the crystal water. She looked over the edge of the boat and spotted large boulders looming up toward them. She'd never seen water so clear.

"How deep is this?"

"One hundred sixty-five feet. Give or take."

He glanced her way, but his eyes were hidden behind mirrored glasses so she couldn't read him. She hoped he took them off because she loved looking into the gorgeous blue depths. She could drown in them. Besides, for this whole seduction thing to work she needed to gauge her progress, and that would be more of a challenge if he were wearing sunglasses.

Whatever. For the moment she leaned back in the seat and tipped her face to the sun. She'd deal with seducing him later.

❦

ARMAND CURSED. Why the hell had he lifted Kayla from the dock and pressed her body to his? He'd been sporting an erection ever since he spied her long, silky-smooth legs clad in short denim. Actually, he questioned why he'd invited her on this excursion but he knew the answer. She was beautiful, sexy and vulnerable and he was a fucking prick who wanted to get laid. For some godforsaken reason guilt ate at him, but he shoved it down. When her body touched his it was like ice sliding along hot steel and he wanted her coolness pressed against his naked, hot flesh. He also wanted the curse broken and if there was even the slightest chance she was the key, he'd take it.

He maneuvered the boat to his favorite spot and let the motor idle while he tossed the anchor off the back to hold the craft in place. "We're here." He turned off the engine and began gathering the cooler and plastic tote to lower them into the water.

"Can I help?"

"We're going to wade in and float these"— he pointed to their cargo—"to shore. The water's only about waist deep here, but if you have your suit on you might want to leave your clothes here." Dear God, did he ever want her to leave her clothes on the boat. Every last stitch.

She nodded and reached for the hem on her shirt, pulled it over her head and tossed it onto the seat. Mounds of golden flesh spilled out of a red bikini top and tempted him. *Holy mother of all that is sacred.* His fingers actually itched with the need to trace a line where flesh met fabric, and his lips wanted to taste every inch of skin then wrap around her sweet nipple and suckle until she moaned his name.

Kayla didn't stop. Next, she unbuttoned her shorts and lowered the zipper. He suppressed a groan as she slid the material past her hips and down her thighs. If that wasn't enough, she kicked them aside and now stood before him in two pieces of red material. Scanty material at best.

"I'm ready," she announced.

Right. So was he. Ready, willing and fucking able and the erection pressing ever so painfully against his shorts was a clear reminder.

Armand lifted his shirt and pulled it over his head, laying it on the back of his seat. Two could play the game of tease. He was a fucking Jinn after all and seduction part of his DNA. Even without any power, no woman had ever been able to resist his body or his charm. He watched her eyes roam down his chest and to the top of his jeans. She drew her lip through her teeth as her gaze lingered. Was she waiting for him to undo the button? Before he could oblige her, she looked up.

"Nice tattoo." She moved to the ladder and proceeded to climb down into the water. "If you want to hand me something, I'll take it to shore."

"Thanks." He grabbed the cooler and plopped it in the water. "I'll be along in a moment. Got some things to finish up first." Like adjusting his throbbing erection. She may have thought she appeared nonchalant, but he could smell her arousal. He'd be willing to bet her bathing suit was wet long before she hit the water.

He fiddled around and tried to look busy while he watched her move to shore from behind his mirrored glasses. She walked up the beach, her bottom half soaked and droplets of water ran down her thighs. He let a moan escape. She had moved too far away to hear him anyway.

"This is going to be a long, fucking day," he growled under his breath then jumped in the water pulling the tote with the rest of their stuff behind him. At least the coolness of the lake assisted in deflating his dick. For the moment.

He detached the two beach chairs he'd brought from the top of the tote and unfolded them. Kayla sidled up next to him, so close he could feel her coolness slide across his skin. *Shit.* He gritted his teeth, needing something to keep himself in check, or he was going to lose all control.

"What can I do?"

He handed her the towels. "You can take these and I'll set up the table."

"Okay." She spun and walked away from him with a little more swing in her hips then she had before.

Son of a bitch! The vixen wants to play does she?

He took the table from the tote, pulled it from its bag and unrolled it. He screwed the legs on and flipped it over.

"Wow, that's cool. I've never seen one of those before." She stood over him. He slipped the glasses off and let his gaze roam up her legs to her stomach and finally to her face.

"I must say, *querida,* that bikini suits you well. You are, eh, most pleasant to look at." He flashed a wide smile and watched her take two steps back.

"Um, thanks."

Was she having second thoughts? Too late, he'd already determined seduction was in the air tonight. He would have her. Not tonight, however. He decided he would make her beg him. When she came to him, she would be unable to stand it any longer and only then would he give her what she needed.

CHAPTER FIVE

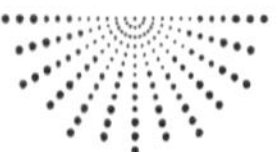

*H*ad he called her darling? Kayla was pretty sure she understood him with what little Spanish she'd learned. Then there was the look in his eyes—as if he wanted to devour her. No woman would mistake it and it had been the confirmation she needed.

He was taking the bait.

She worried slightly though. It had been a long time since she'd had sex. Would he think her inadequate? She had to remind herself this was going to be only a brief encounter. It would end when she went home if not before.

Sex. This was strictly for the sex.

With that in mind, she seated herself in one of the chairs and watched Armand pull a bottle of white wine from the cooler and two glasses from a wicker basket he'd taken out of the tote.

"Would you care for some wine?"

"I'd love some." A little liquid courage certainly couldn't hurt. "So does the tattoo mean anything? " She stared at the thick black bands that wrapped around his right bicep and wanted to trace the markings with her fingers. Instead, she watched him pour the glass to half full with white wine then procure a bottle of water from the cooler. He placed them on the table next to her.

"Not really. It's called a tribal tattoo and I simply liked it. Be sure to drink plenty of water while we're out here so you don't get dehydrated."

Kayla hid a smile behind her hand. "Okay."

He arched a brow. "What are you laughing at?"

"Nothing," she giggled.

"Really? People usually don't laugh at nothing."

She couldn't contain herself any longer and burst into a fit of laughter. "Oh my god. You sound like my dad." She held a hand to her side, unsure of why she'd found it so funny. *Must be nerves.* Armand looked at her with a gleam in his eye, but his face remained stoic. Oh dear, had she upset him? She opened her mouth to apologize when he let out his own hearty laugh.

"I guess that did sound rather fatherly." He moved his chair from the other side of the table up next to hers. "Let me find a subject that is less … parental." He sipped his wine. "So, tell me about your books. I'm curious to know how you come up with those steamy sex scenes." He leaned in closer. "Do you take lots of cold showers?"

At that moment, she wanted to run for the lake and take a dunk. His naked chest stirred things in her that had long been dead. She cleared her throat. "What makes you think I write steamy sex?"

His lips curled into a grin that would melt any woman's panties. "I took the liberty of searching for your work on Amazon and read your first book last night."

All kinds of replies ran through her mind. Discussing the topic with her friends or even her fans was something she did all the time, but to talk about the burning sex she wrote with this hot Spaniard? Her stomach clenched tight at the thought of it so she reached for her wine and took a gulp. He had opened the door, and now she either walked through or slammed it shut and ran the other way.

"Yes. Writing those required lots of freezing showers. Later though, I met my husband and, well, that helped." Not really. If she looked back on her relationship with Eric, he never satisfied her. She always had an empty spot; something was missing, but she never knew what.

He leaned back as if satisfied with her answer and stared at the sky. After a long pause, he looked at her. "You mentioned before not being able to write since your divorce." He ran his finger down her arm and stopped at her wrist, taking it in his grip. "Tell me *querida,* when was the last time a man caressed you?"

Her chest tightened and her breath hitched. A trail of heat still burned where his fingers had slid across her skin. "Ah … " She stared into her lap, unable to look at him. His hand moved away from her wrist and touched her chin. He turned her head to face him, his thumb stroking her cheek.

"Don't hide, Kayla. You're a beautiful woman and there is no reason for you to be alone."

She quivered. God knew she was tired of being by herself and his touch ignited so many things deep inside her. Many of which scared the hell out of her. "Not since my divorce. Two years."

His eyes deepened to the color of midnight. "You deserve better than that, *querida.*" He released her and stood. "How about a swim?"

Good god, yes! Anything to kill the burning currently consuming her. She wasn't used to heat and every time he called her darling in his thick accent she melted. His touch had her heart nearly stopping and she wanted to beg him to continue. Hell, she'd let him take her here in the chair. Her body was strung so tight she feared it might snap at any moment. Had she been surer of herself, she would have pushed him back in his seat, straddled his lap and kissed her way up every hard muscle on his chest until she reached his lips. Those thick, heavy lips. Oh, she would…

"Kayla?"

She blinked. "Huh?" Armand stood beside her his hand held out waiting. *Shit!* She slipped her hand in his and allowed him to help her to her feet. "Sorry."

A mischievous grin formed on his lips. "Quite alright. I'm just curious where you went."

"No place." She'd be damned if she would ever admit what had been running through her mind. For the time being, she'd follow him to the water and douse herself.

ARMAND LED Kayla into the water then swam away. He sensed her distress. She wanted him, the evidence clear, but she feared him at the same time. He blamed it on her lack of sexual activity along with the fact that her bastard husband had cheated on her. That would leave any woman's ego in tatters. The female begged for tenderness. He would give it to her a little at a time until he had tamed the skittish fox and had her eating out of his hand.

He had to admit, though, he admired her. Coming to a foreign country, flirting with a stranger, took courage. It was obvious by her long stint of celibacy, she wasn't the type who slept around and he found that comforting. He'd also been impressed by her writing. While romance wasn't something that lined his bookshelf, he had found her work enjoyable. There was a part of him that wanted to help her get back on her feet. He was certain if she could once again experience the joy of two bodies being together, she'd find her muse. For a moment, sadness filled him. Love was something he'd kept at arm's length and for good reason. He'd watched a few of his elders fall for a human and it always ended in disaster. She would die and they would be left heartbroken, spending eternity watching their offspring perish as well. The gene that made them Jinn never carried on to a human child. It was for the better of their race.

Armand swam for shore and exited the water. "Are you hungry? We should eat since we only have a couple of hours before dark."

He was already in the cooler pulling out the bocata he'd lined with grilled chicken, provolone, arugula and tomato. He laid them on the table then dug for the container of pasta salad.

"I'm starving. What can I do to help?"

Kayla had come up beside him, still drying herself off. He tried to ignore the fact she was running a towel along her wet skin. He wanted to offer his help but fought the urge. He feared moving too fast would scare her off.

"In the basket there are some plates and forks."

"On it." She moved away and dug through the basket producing the items needed and placed them on the table. "Wow, this looks delicious."

Armand parked his chair on the other side of the table. "I hope you like chicken." He unwrapped a sandwich then ladled some pasta salad on a plate and handed it to her. He watched her eyes widen as she accepted it. Had it really been that long since anyone had done something nice for her?

"Thanks." She sat in her chair and took a bite of the sandwich. She moaned. "Oh, my god, this is so good." Next she took a fork full of pasta salad. "Did you make this? I love the olives."

"I picked up the bread from the little bakery we passed on our walk. The rest I made myself. You looked surprised."

"I guess I didn't take you for a cook," she exclaimed.

Armand sat back and watched her eat. "Let me guess. Your husband never cooked for you."

She stopped midway through her pasta salad. "Why would you think that?"

Something told him she wasn't going to admit the guy had treated her badly. He wouldn't push it either. It would only hurt her. He wanted to win her over not scare her away. He shrugged. "In all fairness, being a bachelor has forced me to learn to cook." He smiled at her. "It was either that or rely on the old ladies who took pity on me."

She nodded and continued eating. Her lack of an answer only confirmed his suspicion. He finished his lunch in silence and allowed her to clean up, sensing she needed to busy herself. He wandered off to the water's edge and watched a school of fish jump through the waves. Moments later she stood beside him, her coolness brushed his fire and the urge to pull her to his side had him clenching his fists.

"Thank you for bringing me here. I can see why you love this place. It's so peaceful."

He was taken by surprise when she placed her lips on his cheek and kissed him. He grabbed her by the waist and pressed her to him, unable to resist any longer having her softness pressed against him. "You are so trusting, *querida*. We have only just met and yet you come out to the middle of nowhere with me. How do you know I'm not an animal?" He watched her brown eyes darken and her tongue flick out to wet her lips, her arousal evident by the heavy scent of musk that hung in the air.

"I don't know how to explain it. Something tells me you're not."

If she ever learned what he had once been capable of. He'd killed his enemies and burned their villages. Granted, it had been either his life or theirs, but he'd left many children orphaned. He doubted she would still be so trusting if she knew the truth. No, she would run far away from him and he would be helpless to stop her.

He released her. "We should return home. I'll grab the things and load the boat."

6

CHAPTER SIX

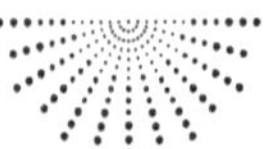

akayla had been positive Armand was going to kiss her. Instead he'd set her aside and almost seemed angry that she had trusted him. Their ride back to the mainland had been quiet and almost tense. What had caused the sudden change? The kiss on the cheek? Everything had certainly gone to hell after that, but she could have sworn he wanted her.

She brushed the hair from her face. What did she know about men anyway? It had been two years since her last relationship and it had failed. She had failed. The entire idea was a mistake and she should just chalk it up to a lesson learned and move on. Tears stung her eyes. She thought she saw something good and decent in Armand. Even if only for a one-night stand, she thought he would have catered to her every need, giving her something her past relationships always lacked. Maybe she should just hire the deed done. Women did it all the time now and why not? Their sexual urges were the same as a man's, only the rules were different.

Half an hour later, they were back at the dock and Armand helped her off the boat.

"I'll escort you home."

Really? She pursed her lips. "I'm sure you have lots to do. I can see myself home. Thank you again for a nice day." She spun and started to walk away, but he was on her heels.

"I wasn't asking." He moved in beside her.

Kayla kept her gaze ahead. She could feel the heat rising up her neck. "Suit yourself." If he wanted to walk with her then fine, but she refused to converse with him. The mixed signals he kept sending were making her dizzy. He went from seductive to demanding to angry with god-knows-what. The confusion running through her brain gave her a headache.

Ten silent minutes later, she finally reached her front door. She slipped the key into the lock and turned the handle. The door opened to reveal a darkened room and she could hardly wait to escape back into it. She wondered if the entire trip was a waste. Good manners had her turning around to face the sexy man who'd towered beside her all day.

"Thank you again. It was lovely."

His hands gripped her upper arms and his body pinned her against the doorjamb. His lips crashed down on hers. Bruising. Demanding. His tongue pushed passed and swept into her mouth. He tasted of danger and sin and she wanted to swallow him whole. Every lean hard muscle of his chest pushed into her breasts causing them to ache. Her nipples pebbled against her bathing suit and begged to have his hot tongue glide across them. His erection, thick and hard, pressed into her belly. She wanted to touch him, but with her arms pinned at her side she could do nothing except remind herself to breathe.

He consumed her.

Armand nipped her bottom lip then pulled away causing her to moan. Even in the dusk of the evening, she could see the desire in his eyes. It burned her soul.

"*Querida,* never trust a strange man again. I will be your one exception," he whispered. "Do you understand?"

She swallowed. Her throat parched from the inferno brewing inside her like a wicked storm. "Y—Yes."

"Good." He released her then backed away. "Go inside now. I'll pick you up tomorrow evening for dinner."

"O—Okay."

Kayla stepped past the entry and closed the door behind her. She leaned against the cool wood both to quench the fire that raged within and for support. She brought her fingers to her swollen lips and could almost feel him still pressing against her.

"What the hell just happened?"

Her legs were like Jell-O and her heart raced. She hadn't expected him to kiss her. Not after the way things had ended. Even in her surprise, her body couldn't help but respond. She had never been kissed like that before. It had been raw. His heat had seeped through her skin igniting something deep inside her.

"So that's what it's like? Holy hell." She pushed herself off the door and walked across the living room on wobbly legs. She needed a cold shower. Ice cold to be exact.

MAKAYLA SAT at the kitchen table and stared at the white page on her laptop. After taking an exceptionally long shower, she decided to see if her muse would cooperate. Her core was still ablaze from Armand's heat when suddenly she remembered.

"Nana. Shit," she whispered.

The words came flooding back to her. *One day Makayla, a special man will ignite the flame within you. However, he will not be who he seems and you'll be forced to make a hard choice.*

There had been more, but it was still fuzzy. She rubbed her temples, trying to remember. She'd been a little girl at the time and Nana had died a few years later. It was peculiar that the Spaniard had been the only man to ever heat her to the bone. Not even Eric had been enough to warm her frigid marrow. Could her crazy nana have been right? Kayla had always believed there was that one special person out there for everyone. Eric was supposed to be hers, but that had turned out to be a joke. Nana had died shortly after she'd married him, but had made it well known to Kayla that she didn't approve of her new husband. She'd even gone so far as to tell her that he'd break her heart.

She rubbed her hands together; the chill had returned. Taking a deep breath, she let the air escape through her mouth, closed her eyes and remembered the kiss. Long, hot and so damn sensual. Christ, what would Armand be like in bed? Would he be the gentleman whom she had first met? Or the man who pinned her against the door? The one who had branded himself on her soul? She decided she yearned for the latter.

Kayla reined in her thoughts and began typing as a story finally unfolded in her mind. Her fingers flew over the keys and she wondered if a mere kiss did this to her, what would having sex with him produce?

A crash behind her had her jumping from the chair and clutching her chest.

"What the … ?"

The vase lay smashed into tiny fragments on the floor and the flowers Armand had brought her on his first visit were ripped to shreds. Kayla looked around the dimly lit room and saw nothing else out of place. She moved to the closet, grabbed a broom and dustpan and began sweeping up the mess. She noticed a nearby window open and wondered if the breeze could have knocked over the vase. However, it didn't explain how the flowers were shredded.

"I really liked those flowers too," she mumbled to herself as she dumped the contents into the trash.

After she placed the broom and pan back into the closet, she glanced at the clock. Ten p.m. It had been a long day so she turned off her laptop and headed for bed. A good night's sleep then she had all day tomorrow to work on her manuscript.

A chill sent her crawling under the covers, her mind flashed back to Armand and she found herself wondering if he was lying in bed at that moment. Did he sleep in the nude? Her skin warmed at the thought.

She tried to analyze his comment to her before he left. *I will be your one exception.* It made no sense to her and then she remembered he had told her he would pick her up for dinner. *Crap!* He hadn't said where they were going so she had no idea if she should wear a dress or jeans. Her mind reeled over the minor details when the blankets were suddenly jerked off her body.

Kayla bolted upright. "H–Hello? Whose there?"

The only reply came from the crickets outside her window. She reached for the cell phone on the nightstand and pressed the button to bring the light on. She quickly located the app for the flashlight and turned it on, shining it from one corner to the other.

Empty.

She ran across the room and flipped on the light switch. The blanket and sheet, previously covering her body, lay in a heap at the foot of the bed. She swallowed down the lump of fear and again searched the room, not even sure what she expected to find. She wondered if she should check the rest of the house then decided against it. Instead, she gathered up the bedding, remade the bed and chalked it up to the day in general and being overly tired. Minutes later she had the light off and was back in bed. Her lids grew heavy and sleep overcame her.

CHAPTER SEVEN

*A*rmand had spent the day preparing for his dinner with Kayla, but the only thing that occupied his mind was their burning kiss. He'd meant to be gentle, but his lust had driven him to pin her and take what he wanted. The coolness of her skin next to his had been like a swim on a hot summer's day and he had wanted to drown in it. For centuries, he'd felt like he was burning alive and suddenly some slip of a female shows up and soothes the flame.

It both perplexed him and pissed him off. Something had snapped when he'd kissed her and the thought of any man ever touching her again had set him on edge. He'd nearly uttered the words, "You belong to me." Yet he'd managed to reel in his desire and walk away. Tonight however, things might prove different.

Armand stepped out the door and looked to the darkened sky. He decided to take the Ferrari to go pick her up just in case of bad weather. He wondered if she would approve of his choice of car. Women liked fast cars.

He whipped out of the driveway and headed down the street. Within minutes, he arrived at her villa and realized he was impatient to see her again. He knocked, listened for her footsteps and waited for the door to open. Even in a simple pair of jeans and top, she stole his breath. She'd left her dark hair loose around her shoulders. Damn, if he didn't want to slide his fingers through it, fist it in his hand, pull her head back and kiss her like his life depended on it. Something in his gut told him his life may well depend on it.

"Hi. Come on in." She grinned at him and started to move aside when her eyes widened. "Wow. Is that your car?"

Yes. The reaction he'd hoped for. "It is. I thought since it looked like rain I'd drive."

She stepped out of the way to let him enter. "Oh, I can't wait to see the inside. I've never been in a Ferrari before. Hell, I've not even been close to one." She shut the door. "Oh and thanks for calling me this morning. I really had no idea if I was to wear jeans or a ball gown for dinner." She let out a light laugh.

He couldn't help but chuckle and was glad to see her sense of humor returning. "Do you own a ball gown?"

She rolled her eyes. "No, so I was really happy when you said casual." She tucked a piece of hair behind her ear. "Let me grab my purse and we can go."

She walked over to the kitchen table and it was then he noticed something missing. The flowers he'd given her were not sitting on the counter. Had she tossed them out? He knew she had been ticked at him last night, but she didn't seem like the kind of person who'd do that. He was usually a good judge of character, but then again he didn't know her all that well. He'd find out in his own way before the end of the night.

"I'm ready."

"Good. Are you hungry?" He strode to the door and waited for her to exit before he closed it, making sure it was securely locked behind him.

"I'm starved. I forgot to eat lunch today."

He skirted around her but not before taking a moment to admire her firm ass. Damn, if it didn't look as good in denim as it had in a bikini. He opened the car door and motioned for her to enter. After she folded into the seat, he shut the door and hurried around to the driver's side. Once inside, he turned over the engine and backed out of the driveway.

"This is really nice." She caressed the counsel. His cock stirred.

Focus you fucking idiot. Now was not the time for thinking about her hands all over him. "When the weather is nicer, I'll take you for a ride through the mountains. It's a rush."

She stared at him, her brown eyes sparked with interest. "Oh, that sounds like fun."

"So tell me, what kept you so busy you forgot to eat?"

She turned away from him and looked out the window. The rain began to splatter small drops on the glass. "I was busy writing."

"That's wonderful news! So what do you suppose inspired you? Was it the beauty of our country?"

She turned from the window only to stare straight ahead. "Yes. It is beautiful here, how could an artist not be inspired?"

Interesting, she seemed to avoid looking directly at him. "What about the kiss, *querida?* Did my passion inspire you at all?" He waited, needing to know how she would answer.

"Is your ego really that big?" The slight twinge at the corner of her lips showed her amusement. Fine, he'd play along and see where it led.

"Of course. I'm a man and need to know if I pleased you." He pulled into his driveway and pressed the button to open the garage.

She shrugged her shoulders. "It was fine."

He pressed his palm to his heart feigning hurt. "I endeavor to do better then. Perhaps you'll let me try again?"

She broke into a full-blown smile. "Perhaps."

That was all he needed and he pulled into the garage to park the car. In seconds, he had her door opened. "Welcome to my home. Come in and let me give you the tour."

MAKAYLA STEPPED from the car enjoying the cat and mouse game she'd just played with Armand. She'd wanted to tell him his kiss was perfect. The best she'd ever had and if she were never kissed like that again she would always treasure that one time with him. However, her needy side wanted another. The woman in her that had been neglected for so long desired much more than a kiss. She was already painfully aware it wouldn't take much for him to get her into his bed. After all, she'd started the game and now prayed he would finish it.

She stepped through the wooden door he held open and gasped. She'd expected grand when they'd pulled into the driveway. However, this was beyond any words she could form. She stood in the entry of a kitchen three times bigger than her apartment back home. Warm oak cabinets lined one side of the room with two stainless steel built-in ovens. There were two islands, one in the middle with a small sink for prep work, and the other with seats for eating separated a small family area that held a couch, two chairs and a large flat screen TV. When she looked up, the skylight-filled ceiling went on forever. Even with its sheer size it left her feeling warm, and she could see herself busy preparing meals here.

He tossed his keys in an orange ceramic bowl on the counter. "My home is your home. Would you like to see the rest?"

"Oh, yes please!" What were the chances she'd ever be in a house so luxurious again? She wanted to soak in every detail and file it away for future reference.

He placed his palm at the small of her back, melting away the layers of ice. Nana's words echoed in her head and she couldn't help but think there might be something to them.

"Wonderful. We'll move to the living area next."

He ushered her through a high archway where the floor changed from terra cotta colored tile to warm oak with a sheen so polished it almost looked like glass. Looking at the recessed windows and skylights that dotted the ceiling, Kayla could only imagine what the room would look like on a sunny day.

On the other side, another archway made of glass with large French doors led outside to a swimming pool. Armand quickly led her through the rec room, a home theater and several others until her head spun.

"This is the room I wanted you to see." His voice dropped to a low seductive level.

She realized they had entered a bedroom. Kayla scanned the large master suite with a king size bed. His bed? She quickly turned her attention to the room on the other side and walked through the archway. She'd never seen a bathroom so large. Hell, the walk in shower alone would fit most of a football team.

She let out a squeal and moved to the alcove, running her hand over the smooth white porcelain of the tub tucked so nicely in the space and surrounded by windows. She imagined bubble baths while sipping wine. She also couldn't help notice it was big enough for two.

"Dear god, I've never seen anything like this house before. It really is beautiful." She knew she should be nervous standing in the room where he slept, but instead had the urge to fling open his closets and see his wardrobe. Clothes and how they were kept said a lot about a man. She could picture his things all neatly folded with everything having its proper place.

Kayla wondered if he was going to kiss her again and her cheeks heated.

"I'm glad you approve. Now let's go have some dinner."

Armand led her back through the house to the dining area where candles lit the table and flowers filled a vase in the center. She tried to hide her disappointment that he hadn't kissed her and wondered if she should become the initiator? Perhaps after dinner.

She gazed at the flowers and they reminded her of the ones he'd given her that now sat in the trash. A pang of guilt rushed through her. Not that it had been her fault, but she was still edgy from last night's events. The real reason she'd missed lunch was because she had fallen asleep.

"Kayla?"

She jumped. "Oh. Sorry." Armand had pulled out a chair at the table and waited for her to be seated.

"What is bothering you, *querida?* You seem so far away tonight." He pushed her chair in once she had sat, filled her wine glass then took the seat next to her. His intense blue stare bore into her. He was going to insist she open up.

"You'll think I'm an absolute nut job."

"Try me. I think you'll find I'm very open minded." He crossed his arms over his chest and arched a brow.

"Fine. After you walked me home, I showered then went to the kitchen table to write. I was deep in thought when I heard a crash." She picked at the hem of her shirt.

He leaned forward and placed his hand over hers. "You're fidgeting."

She looked up and met his gaze. God, how she loved staring into his eyes, felt like she could live there. It was then she realized she was falling for him. *This can't be happening. It's too fast. But he makes me feel so safe.*

"Kayla." Armand tapped his fingers on the table.

"Right. When I turned around to see what happened, the vase of flowers was on the floor."

He leaned back and appeared more relaxed. "I'm sure the wind knocked them over. Don't worry, my gardens have plenty of flowers and you shall have a fresh bouquet everyday."

He started to rise, but she touched his arm. "No, that's not all." He sat back in his chair. "I thought the same thing, but the flowers were in tatters as if something had ripped them apart. There is no way the wind could do that."

He rubbed the stubble on his jaw. "There is more?"

"Yes. After I went to bed, I was nearly asleep when the covers were jerked off me. When I turned on the light, they were crumpled up at the foot of the bed. This happened twice so I finally gave up trying to sleep."

"Most peculiar. Let me think about this while we eat." He rose and left the room. Kayla wondered what was going through his mind at the moment. Did he think her a real nut case and was just being kind in not telling her?

CHAPTER EIGHT

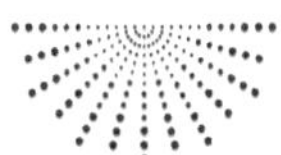

*A*lthough pleased Kayla enjoyed the dinner he'd prepared, Armand couldn't help think about what had happened at her place last night. She seemed fine other than a bit on edge, but that was to be expected. He knew some of the homes here were haunted. Old souls often refused to move on, but none had proved harmful to those they encountered.

"Are you sure you got enough to eat?" he inquired.

She placed a hand on her stomach. "I am stuffed. Those were some of the best *tapas* I've ever eaten."

"Good, I'm happy to hear that." He handed her a glass of wine then joined her on the sofa in front of the fireplace. It was too warm to light so he'd placed several candles in the hearth. "This storm is really picking up. We may lose power."

She took a sip from her glass. "Does that happen often?"

No sooner had the words crossed her lips than a loud clap of thunder rattled the windows and everything went dark. All that remained were a few flickering candles.

"Wow. If I didn't know better, I'd say you planned that." She set her glass on the side table and leaned closer to him. "I love storms. There's just something about them that makes me want to snuggle in."

Even with his power, he couldn't control the weather so he was grateful as hell to Mother Nature for obliging him. He slipped his arm around Kayla's shoulder and pulled her closer. "Snuggle in then. I have plenty of wine and lots of candles."

"Tell me, do you believe in ghosts?" He gauged her reaction.

"I guess. Are going to tell me my little villa is haunted?"

"It has been known to happen. Many strange things occur in our ancient village." He squeezed her shoulder. "There is even a belief that the Jinn once lived here."

Kayla broke away and stared at him, her body stiff. This appeared to be a touchy subject and he needed to know why.

"You don't believe in the supernatural?"

She flicked out her tongue and licked her lips. He could focus on nothing else but her mouth and how desperate he was to taste her again.

"Of course there are things we can't explain. I believe in spirits, but Jinn are a myth just like vampires and shape-shifters."

Why did he not believe her? Something in her eyes said she wanted to, but would need proof. Never had he wanted his power more. The desire for her to know who and what he was burned his soul. He had tired of his lonely existence. Yes, he had an entire village yet he had to hide his identity. He wanted the woman who sat next to him to know the truth, but he had nothing to back up his claim. Instead, he smiled at her. "Yes, they are only a myth." The words stung. *I must be a fucking fool! I can't have her in that way. She is mortal.*

Kayla settled back and laid her head on his shoulder, but when she tipped her chin to look up at him, his barriers broke down. He leaned closer and brushed his lips across hers in a gentle sweep then pulled away.

She moaned then licked her lips. "Don't stop."

No more encouragement was needed. He slipped his fingers through her hair and gripped a handful and nibbled her bottom lip. Gods, she tasted like strawberries and cream and he wanted more. He wanted all of her. He thrust his tongue in her mouth and she wrapped her arms around his neck pulling him closer. He could feel his internal temperature rising and her biting chill only fueled his Jinn. If he had his magic, he'd take her to the most beautiful places on earth. He even found himself wanting to take her home and share with her his world.

Before he knew it, he pushed her backward, or had she pulled him? It didn't matter. She lay back on the couch and he rested on top of her, careful not to crush her. She entwined a leg around his. He broke the kiss and leaned back slightly to look at her.

"*Querida*, I am finding you hard to resist." If she allowed him, he would take her right now. Hard and fast, then later slow and easy. Never had he desired a woman more.

Makayla blinked and wondered why Armand stopped kissing her to talk. She wanted more lip action like what he'd just given her. Good god, but her entire body hummed. There was no stopping, no going back. She wanted to be consumed by him and for Christ's sake, she needed him to ease the ache that beat like a drum between her legs.

"If you find me hard to resist, then why did you stop kissing me?"

He leaned further away from her. *Oh shit.* Were they going down that road again? Would she ever get laid?

"Because if I continue kissing you like this … I won't stop there." He brushed some stray hair from her eyes. "I need to know what it is you want from this night."

She thought for a moment and admired him for thinking of her. The kind Armand was showing himself, but she wanted to see the other side again. Now she had to figure out how to explain her deepest desire.

"You're not talking," he stated.

"I'm not sure how to say it," she whispered.

"You can tell me anything. If you wish to leave here now and go home, then I will take you. If you desire something else, please share it with me." He brushed his finger down her arm.

"I want you, Armand." She closed her eyes and tried to dig for her courage, but it didn't stop the tears from escaping. "For once in my life, I want to be the center of a man's attention." She was afraid to look at him but did so anyway. "I know it sounds stupid, but I want to know what it's like to be the heroine." If he'd really read any of her work, he would know to what she referred.

Armand stood. He held out his hand and her heart sank. He thought she was a fool and was going to drive her home. Probably just as well. It would be best to end this before she made an even bigger idiot of herself. She accepted his hand and stood ready to face him with dignity when he jerked her to his hardened chest and pressed his lips against her ear.

"Feel my erection digging into you, *querida?* This is what you do to me." He suckled her lobe. "I'm going to make you come so many times, you'll forget your name."

She whimpered.

He released her and grabbed the hem of his shirt. Slowly he teased her as he raised the fabric up exposing his hard abs, then his chest.

She licked her lips, remembering what he looked like and desperate to see him totally naked.

The shirt was pulled over his head then tossed to the floor. He reached for the snap on his jeans and his hair fell into his face. He peered at her, through dark brown locks, looking of danger and sex all rolled into one smoking hot package.

Armand popped the button and lowered the zipper.

Kayla chewed her bottom lip. Her pulse raced and she couldn't take her eyes off him, wanting to see what hid behind the denim. She didn't have long to wait as he lowered his jeans past his hips and pushed them to the floor. He stepped free of the pile and kicked it aside. He stood before her like a Greek god. His erection a thing of beauty, thick and long, she wondered if her hand would be able to encompass its girth.

She ached to run her fingers over each defined muscle followed by her tongue. Kayla could scarcely believe she was about to have sex with this man. Moisture pooled and her pulse pounded at her apex.

He stood with his arms at his side. "Come to me, *querida*." A command that wasn't to be disobeyed.

Placing one foot in front of the other, she moved in closer. Being in his personal space brought on a sudden rush of anxiety. Dare she touch him? She almost felt like she needed permission. "Dear god, Armand. You are absolutely everything a woman dreams of."

"*Eres tan preciosa.*" He wrapped his hand around the back of her neck and pulled her into him.

She shuddered both from his possessiveness and his thick accent. If she didn't melt into a pool on the floor, it would indeed be a miracle. "What does that mean?"

"You are so beautiful." He kissed her neck. "These clothes of yours must go."

With his free hand, he grabbed the hem of her tee and slid it up her body. She wasn't sure how, but he managed to remove it within seconds and toss it with the others. He kissed his way down her neck and across the tops of her breasts. He cupped each one and gave a light squeeze then sucked a nipple through the fabric of her bra.

Her knees buckled.

The only thing keeping her standing was his arm around her waist. Armand moved to the other breast and gave it the same loving attention before he unsnapped her jeans then lowered the zipper. Before she knew it, they met the same fate as the shirt and she was left in only her bra and panties.

He leaned back. "Ah, *querida*. You are a goddess to be worshipped and I intend to do so from one end of this room to the other."

"I … " She couldn't form words.

Armand lifted her and laid her on the couch, kissed her knuckles then up her arm until he reached the sensitive part at the top of her shoulder.

She shivered but not from the cold. She'd never been hotter in her life.

He slipped his hand past the elastic of her panties and ran a finger through her wetness. She arched her hips to beg for more.

He gently bit her nipple through her bra as he inserted a finger into her sheath.

She sucked in a breath. Nothing had ever felt better and she craved more, wanted all of him. He inserted a second finger. She gyrated and thrust against his hand. Within seconds her first orgasm rushed over her. Her entire body tensed before relaxing again. Armand kissed her. Lips soft and gentle before pulling away.

"That was only the beginning," he whispered.

Makayla tried to catch her breath. "I—I'm not sure I can move."

The candlelight reflected off his face and revealed a sexy grin. "No need to move just yet." He pushed the straps of her bra down her arms then reached behind her, lifting her slightly to unhook the clasp. He slid the fabric off her breasts and tossed it in the air. *"Perfección!"* He ran his tongue across her nipple.

She dug her fingers into his thick hair and pressed him to her. "Armand." He seemed to know exactly how to stoke her fire. He sucked the hardened protrusion into his mouth and swirled his tongue around it before breaking free, leaving her with a deep ache she feared would never be sated.

He kissed his way along her stomach, grabbed her panties and pulled them down her hips while his tongue left a hot trail on the inside of her thigh, then along her calf. He spread her legs and repeated the heated process up the other leg until he reached her apex.

Her breath hitched; her heart sped up.

Armand blew his hot breath over her swollen nub. She sucked air into her lungs and held it. Time stood still while she waited. Then came the first swipe of his tongue, sending liquid fire through her veins and a desire so deep she wanted to beg him to fill her.

He lapped at her like a starved man. His tongue darted in and out of her sheath driving her to the edge of insanity. Her orgasm felt so close she could almost touch it, but it hung back. He teased and tortured her.

She clenched her jaw.

"Oh God, I'm so close. Please ... Please, don't stop."

Armand sucked her nub into his mouth and she skyrocketed. Stars exploded behind her eyes as her orgasm consumed her entire body. Wave, after earth-shattering wave carried her to heights she never knew existed. Kayla couldn't help wonder if her body responded this way now, how wonderful it would be to have him inside her. Even after her mind had just been blown away, she couldn't wait to find out.

"Armand, I need you inside me." She could hardly speak, her throat parched from the inferno that burned inside her.

CHAPTER NINE

The words he'd been waiting to hear. Armand wanted nothing more than to be buried deep inside Kayla. Her orgasm had brought him more pleasure than anything had in a long time. Being earth bound for so long led to major boredom, and there were only so many ways to alleviate it. He scooped her up in his arms, sat on the couch and planted her on his lap.

He produced a foil packet and tore it open. The last thing he wanted was to get her with child. He removed the condom and rolled it over his cock.

"Take me when you are ready, *querida,*" he whispered then cupped her face and pulled her in for a brief kiss. He watched, breathless as she poised herself over him. Slowly, she lowered down onto his shaft. Giving control was not something he was used to, but he felt she needed it, and he would give her anything. Her tears had cut through him like shards of glass and he vowed to give her what she so desperately desired. Something her ex had not, and for that he wanted to kill him.

He dug his nails into his palms to keep from gripping her hips and shoving himself deep. The desire to feel her sheath surrounding his cock blurred his vision. Heat released from his body and the coolness of her enveloped him. She was like a cold drink of water.

Kayla leaned over him, her hands on his chest and the most intense look of pleasure on her face. She settled herself on him firmly to the hilt. "Armand. Damn this feels so good. I—" She shuddered.

"I can say the same." He gripped her hips and held her firm against him wanting to hold onto the feeling for a moment longer. "Kayla, I'm fighting my urges."

She kissed his chest. "What urges would that be?"

"The primal ones that want you fast and hard." He let out a moan when she slid herself up and then down again. It was sheer torture.

"Why fight them?" She whispered between peppered kisses to his flesh.

"I want to give you gentle. You deserve at least that much."

She looked up and met his gaze. Her black hair fell into her face; her dark eyes sparked with fire. She was the sexiest woman he had ever seen. "Show me who you really are, Armand. I want to experience the man who kissed me last night. I won't break." She rocked her hips sending the point home.

In a flash, he had her on the floor, arms pinned over her head as he slid inside her heat. "Are you sure? I will own every inch of your body, *querida.*"

"I've never been more certain. Please, show me what it's like."

He kissed the top of her breast. Swirled his tongue around her nipple then gave it a light nip before sucking it into his mouth to savor. She moaned beneath him and the sound had him thrusting his hips. He moved to her mouth and pushed his tongue passed her lips. He swiped and tasted every inch of her, consuming her, and she responded by lifting her hips to meet his. She was full of passion and desire and his Jinn stirred deep inside him. It ached to be released from centuries of confinement.

Droplets formed on his brow as the magic swirled, looking for an escape. Pressure built in his groin and semen rose, filling the woman beneath him. He threw his head back and roared as the orgasm swept over his body and the magic burned him. He thought he heard Kayla cry out through the haze that surrounded him. When the waves of pleasure finally subsided, he wrapped his arms around her and brought her to his chest. In that moment, he almost wished time would stand still so he could enjoy it for eternity. It wasn't to be. Something stirred deep inside of him and he was helpless to stop it.

❀

MAKAYLA RUBBED her hands across Armand's strong back. She loved the feel of him inside her, on top of her and wanted to stay that way forever. For the first time in her life, she felt warm and liked it. There was something else though. A piece of her heart had been torn away when he entered her and she knew she would never get it back. No matter what happened between them, Armand would always have it.

She wondered if this had been what her nana had been trying to tell her. Was Armand the man she spoke of? If so, what had she meant by he wasn't what he seemed? Kayla sighed. *It figures I'd fall in love with him. Watch him turn out to be a nut case.*

Querida, are you all right?" Armand lifted himself and peered into her eyes.

She curled her lips and wondered if the smile covered her entire face. "Never better." She palmed his cheek and he closed his eyes nuzzling into her until his eyes flew open and she saw panic residing in their blue depths.

"Son of a bitch!" Armand pulled free from her and jumped to his feet.

She sat up. "What's wrong? Armand?" Kayla stood and approached him, his body visibly shaking. "Armand, what do you need me to do? Shall I get help?" She'd never felt more helpless in her life.

"Kayla. Stand back."

Hearing the desperation in his voice, she obeyed.

"I promise I'll never hurt you." He jerked his head back and yelled as if in pain.

Kayla reached for her clothes. "Armand, you're scaring the hell out of me."

His body contorted and black smoked swirled around him until it reached the ceiling, where it snaked back down and headed for the fireplace. It twisted into a thin stream and shot up the chimney. Kayla's heart pounded and she turned around to where Armand had been engulfed in the smoke.

Gone.

"Armand?"

She grabbed her top and slipped it over her head then pulled on her jeans, running through the house while she buttoned them. "Armand?"

No answer, just eerie silence. Even the storms had passed, but the house remained in darkness. She checked every room before heading back to where she started. Still no sign of him. It was like he'd never been there. She plunked down in a chair, dropped her head into her hands and tried to push her panic aside.

"I have no idea what to do."

ARMAND COULD SEE the panic on Kayla's face, but was unable to respond or assure her everything would be fine. At least, he hoped like hell it was. He'd felt the fire ignite deep in his gut and knew the shift was coming but he couldn't stop it. Instead, the vortex overtook him and he turned into his smoke element. The only thing he could think to do was make a hasty exit up the chimney before anything else went awry.

Currently, he floated high above his home trying to regain control. He'd not shifted in over a thousand years and it was both frightening and exhilarating. He feared for Kayla, though, and fought to get back to her. His instinct was to stay in the shift, but his urges were to reunite with her and find out just who the hell she really was and make sure she was safe.

He wrestled for control and reigned in his Jinn. Focusing on the chimney, he shot back through and into the house. He found Kayla sitting on the couch, gulping a glass of wine. Tears stained her face.

"*Querida*, are you harmed?"

"Me? No, but what the hell just happened?" The panic still resided in her voice. He sensed her struggled to remain calm.

"It would seem you have broken the curse. Well, partially anyway," he replied.

She raised a brow. "Care to explain more?" She poured another glass of wine.

Armand took a seat next to her, not bothering to cover his naked body. He tried to focus on her eyes but found it difficult. His gaze kept wandering to her lips. He realized he was desperate to kiss her and wanted the flavor of strawberries to coat his tongue.

"What are you?"

"I am Jinn and I've been cursed to this realm for over a thousand years.

She sucked in a breath. "Jinn? I thought you were only a figment of my nana's imagination." She rubbed her temple. "How were you cursed?"

Armand raised a brow. "Your nana? What was it she told you about us?"

"My great grandmother used to tell me stories of the Jinn. Said there were those who were friend and those who were foe. Which are you?"

He noticed her hands shaking, wrapped his arms around her and pulled her to him. He brought his lips to her temple and kissed the pulse that raced beneath them. The woman who shook in his arms was somehow the key to his release, yet he didn't have the heart to make demands of her. "*Querida*, haven't I already proved which I am? I vow to our gods I would never harm you. I must know, however, how is it your grandmother knew about us?"

She shifted. "I don't really know. I always thought she was crazy. She used to tell me I would one day find a man who would ignite my flame. I never knew what it meant until I met you." She tipped her head to look up at him, licked her lips. "Armand, I have been cold all my life. Even in the middle of a ninety-degree day my hands were like ice. For some reason, when I touch you it warms me. Do you know why that is?"

"I'm not really sure." He had his suspicions and would have Crone check into it on his next visit.

She gave a slight nod. "Tell me about the curse."

He settled back in his seat with her tucked in beside him. "I was young and impressionable and Cyndel was a beautiful genie who seduced me." Kayla's body tensed beside him. "She was a good time, but when she wanted to get serious and marry ... I said no."

"So you used her and she got back at you is pretty much what I'm hearing."

He tipped her chin and looked into her eyes. There was a mix of fear and hunger gazing back at him. He needed this woman and had to make sure he sated both. "I refused to marry her because I didn't love her. Don't pity Cyndel. She only wanted my power and wealth. She was a greedy bitch."

"What about me, Armand. What am I?"

He leaned closer. "You are my salvation." His lips grazed hers. Gentle at first, then demanding. He hungered for every part of her and ran his tongue along the seam of her mouth, which she parted to allow him entry. A burst of strawberries coated his tongue and sent his senses reeling. He broke off and stared into her pools of brown.

"I need you. Do you still trust me, *querida*?"

He waited for her to answer. Fought the urge to kiss her again, to drink in her coolness. She had to need him as well, but most of all he desired her trust.

She placed a hand on his cheek. "Some would think I'm crazy, but I do trust you and God knows I need you as well."

CHAPTER TEN

akayla was fast asleep with her head on Armand's chest and her arm flung across his waist. He'd taken her three more times before they'd finally come to bed. She'd fallen asleep as soon as he laid her on the mattress, and he felt a little guilty for having worn her out. He stared up at the ceiling recalling every moment of the evening.

Making love to her had done something to him. Not since his curse had his magic stirred, but tonight when he had entered her for the first time it had beat at him like a caged animal. He'd lost control and shifted in front of her.

This unsettled him.

Tomorrow, Crone would be coming for his allowed visit and he would have to make sure to tell him what had happened. It meant something, but what he had no clue. Was the curse wearing off? Armand tried to conjure his magic but to no avail. He thought of his internal fire and prayed to shift into smoke, but again nothing happened. He stroked Kayla's hair, enjoying the softness against his hand. His cock came to life, but he pushed back his desire. He had to remind himself she was mortal—another thing that perplexed him. He had never fucked the same human more than once, didn't want to chance getting attached to one. Yet he had made love to her four times and still desired more. He wondered if it was her coolness that soothed him. Could that have been what freed him last night? There was definitely a connection between her and his shifting. She'd also said something about being cold and how he warmed her.

He could have mentioned his thoughts, but for some reason kept them to himself. Somehow he had to figure out how she fit into breaking his curse while still maintaining his emotional distance. The last thing he needed was to fall in love with her.

He closed his eyes and tried to sleep, but realized dawn was approaching. Crone would be here as soon as the sun rose above the horizon. Armand tossed the covers aside then slipped from Kayla's grip.

She stirred, her eyes fluttered open. "Where are you going?"

He leaned over and kissed her head. "I need to shower. I have a meeting in a couple of hours that will keep me all day. You're welcome to stay or I can see you home." He wasn't ready to tell her about his brother coming.

She sat up and stretched. "Mmm. I should go home, I have some things I need to get done." She rolled out of bed. "Do I have time for coffee?"

"Help yourself to anything you find, and please don't rush on my account." Gazing at her naked body had him all jacked up. "*Querida,* the things going through my mind right now. If—" He almost slipped and said if she wasn't human. "If I had more time I'd … "

She strolled around the bed and came up beside him. "I know exactly what I'd do, but the day brings things that need to be done." She touched his cheek and her lips twisted into a smile that lit the entire room. "We have time later. I'll find my clothes then make some coffee." She was out the door before he could say another word. He raced to the shower to hurry and wash up so he had time to join her before they had to part for the day.

❀

KAYLA HAD INSISTED she walk home, stating the fresh air would help clear her mind and get the creative gears turning. She was positive there was a story brewing in her head and after last night, Armand was sure she'd have no trouble with her muse.

"She's a pretty thing."

Armand turned from the window where he watched Kayla walk away and faced his brother, Crone. "Yes she is."

"I wouldn't mind having a go with her myself. Think she'd—"

Armand flew at his brother and pinned him to the wall. "You fucking touch her and I will kill you."

Crone arched a brow. "Really? Have you forgotten you are powerless?" To prove his point, he flicked his wrist and his magic sent Armand flying into the air, stopping his descent inches from crashing into an expensive wooden table. "I'd hate to destroy the furniture." He lowered Armand to his feet.

Armand growled. His arms pinned to his side and his feet firmly planted on the floor. "Release me!"

Crone crossed his arms over his chest. Amusement danced in his eyes. "Not until you behave. I was only joking, but it would seem you are infatuated with this human." Crone gave a sigh. "You have been on earth too long." He released Armand from his magical hold.

Armand crossed back to the window, hoping to catch a glimpse of Kayla descending the hill into town. Her small form could be seen in the distance. He turned around. "Something peculiar happened last night."

Crone picked up a billiard from the table and tossed it in the air. "Such as?"

"While having sex I felt my magic stir. I shifted right in front of Kayla. I had no control over it."

His brother left the pool ball hanging mid-air.

"Have you tried calling it again?" Crone tapped his foot on the floor.

Armand moved to the bar, deciding he needed something stronger than coffee. He grabbed a bottle of whiskey and two glasses then headed for the chair. Crone joined him.

"I have and nothing."

Crone scratched his chin. "Hmm, perhaps the curse is wearing off?"

Armand filled both glasses to half-full and handed one to his brother before sipping from his own. "I wondered the same thing. However, there is more to it." He went on to retell how Kayla had cooled him and it seemed she was warmed by him.

"This is interesting. How do you feel right now?" Crone asked.

"Same as I have my entire existence on earth. Powerless."

His brother's gaze moved to the window across the room. "So the only difference now is the girl."

Armand had racked his brain all night looking for anything he had done differently down to the food he'd eaten. He concluded it had to be Makayla, had known she was somehow special the first time he laid eyes on her, but how he had no idea. "It's beginning to look that way."

"Well then, I can see why she makes you testy. I'll dive into the scripts when I get home."

Armand nodded then tipped his glass back and drained it. Somehow, he had to keep Kayla close to him. Maybe he could get his Jinn to release. "There's only one problem."

Crone arched a brow. "That is?"

"Kayla will be gone from here and back home before you return again."

Crone swirled the liquid in his glass then took a swig. "I don't see that as a problem. If I discover she is the key, then I will find her and bring her back to you. Well, as close as I can anyway." He smiled. "However, it might be to your benefit to try and keep her here. Turn up your charm and make her fall in love with you."

That was the problem. He didn't want to break Kayla's heart. The old Armand, who had been left here a thousand years ago, wouldn't care. That Armand would have taken whatever he wanted. However, time had taught him many things. He'd watched so many people he had come to love pass on to the next world. Then he'd watched their children die. Generation after generation of people he tried not to care for had left him with a gaping hole in his heart.

He was going to have to face a hard truth. If she really did hold the key to unlock his freedom, would he use her to get it? He'd been ready to earlier, but something had changed since the other day. Things were moving too fast.

"Brother?"

He met Crone's narrowed gaze. "Yes?"

"You *will* do whatever is necessary to get home. Your family needs you and it is past time to take your rightful place."

He nodded. "I will do what I must." In his heart, he knew he had no choice.

KAYLA STEPPED through the door to her villa and could swear she had floated all the way home. Last night had been like a dream, and she had to keep pinching herself to make sure it was real. She'd had sex with one of the most gorgeous men ever and to top it off it had been amazing. Her muscles ached in the best way.

She was still having a difficult time wrapping her head around the fact he was a Jinn. However, more memories of her nana's stories about the Jinn were starting to return. Nana had said there was another path Kayla could choose. One that would lead her to a love so strong nothing could break it. It would come at a cost though. Everything did.

She shook her head, desperate to remember everything and make sense of it. Hopefully, it would come back to her. Maybe Armand would come up with something as well and tonight they could compare notes.

Kayla stepped into the bathroom and looked at her reflection in the mirror. Yep, she had a rosy glow. It was amazing what sex could do for a gal's outlook. Nikki had been right to send her here in the hopes she'd loosen up. A quick shower then she'd hit the laptop for some writing.

She turned on the water then stripped and stepped into the warm spray and let it cascade over her. She filled the bath scrunchie with coconut-scented wash then lathered her skin. After a rinse, she filled her hand with shampoo then stopped short of scrubbing it through her hair. Instead she pushed open the glass doors and stuck her head out. She could have sworn she heard a noise.

"Hello?"

Quiet.

She shrugged, shut the door and went back to washing her hair. She was both tired and still in a mental state of shock from last night. Perhaps a nap before she started writing so she could start with a fresh mind.

Kayla exited the shower and wrapped one towel around her head and dried off with the other before she headed to the bedroom. She grabbed a clean pair of shorts and a tank and slipped them on. It dawned on her to go grab a glass of water before hitting the sack. She strolled into the kitchen and stopped short.

"Oh no! No. No."

Her laptop lay in pieces on the floor. She swallowed her fear and glanced around the room. Nothing else broken. The front door was closed and nothing else appeared missing.

Her skin crawled with the feeling that someone was watching her.

"Hello? W—Whose here?"

No reply except a cold breeze that snaked across her and caused her skin to pebble. Her throat tightened like she hadn't drunk in days, she was so parched. She licked her lips.

The cold wrapped around her again, but this time pain followed.

She yelled out.

Something warm trickled down her arm and she glanced where the pain was to find three deep scratches dripping blood. She slapped her hand over the wounds and headed for the sink, but was pushed by an invisible force.

Kayla skidded across the tile floor straight into the kitchen knocking a chair over. The skin on her scalp went tight and an immense force jammed her head into the oak cabinet.

Stars circled around her eyes and she could already feel the right side of her face swelling.

She sucked in a breath through the pain. *Stay awake, Kayla.* Something told her if she passed out she might never wake up. Whatever attacked her was pissed. She wished she knew why. With one thought in mind, she pushed herself to her feet, her hands clutching the counter for support. Bile rose to the back of her throat and her breaths came so fast she feared hyperventilating.

She scanned the room through hazy vision, but saw nothing.

Time to make a run for it.

Kayla sprinted to the bedroom. Her common sense said she should've headed for the front door, but her memories reminded her of Nana and the pendant she'd given her as a child. She could hear the elderly woman's voice telling her to run.

She made it to the door when once again she was shoved with such force she flew across the room and landed in a heap in the corner. Through the fog in her head, an image formed in the doorway. A woman dressed in a black strapless top and a flimsy skirt flashed violet eyes at her. If Kayla hadn't been so beaten and frightened, she might have taken a moment to admire the female's beauty. Black, silky hair flowed down her back and intricate branching tattoos covered one side of her midriff.

"You will die before you take him from me!" The woman screeched at her. Sparks shot from her fingertips

Kayla trembled and wondered, if she closed her eyes and opened them again, would she wake up and find this had only been one helluva nightmare? She dared not try. Her mind focused on one thing.

The pendant.

It was located on the nightstand on the other side of the bed. She only needed to jump from the corner, across the bed and claim it.

What if Nana was wrong? The old woman had been sharp as a tack until the day she died. She'd always told Kayla the pendant would help protect her, but there was a chant that went with using it and that came with a price.

If she spoke the words, she'd not only send the intended into purgatory, she'd gain their power and lose her mortality. She had almost laughed out loud when she heard the story. The whole idea had been ludicrous but in her current situation she'd try anything. Trouble was, she didn't remember the words and the woman descended on her fast.

Kayla sucked in a breath, focused on her prize and leapt for the bed. She heard a loud snap right before pain went shooting through her mid-section. She cried out as she landed on the bed, her muscles refusing to obey. She looked out of the corner of her eye. The woman had to be Cyndel. Who else would want to harm her?

The woman moved closer. "Prepare to die. Human."

Kayla refused to give up. No way in hell she was letting this bitch win. The silver chain dangled over the edge of the nightstand. She willed her arm to stretch out in front of her and could hear the loud pops of electrical current behind her as her fingers made contact with the metal.

She gritted her teeth against the pain and pulled. The pendant broke free and she rolled off the bed just in the nick of time. Smoke rose off the mattress. Kayla pulled the necklace over her head and let the stone settle between her breasts. The woman screeched and vanished in a swirl of smoke. Kayla sat huddled on the floor. Her body shivered and white-hot pain racked her gut. She spotted her phone on the nightstand and reached for it. Her limbs so weak she dropped it, but luckily it fell right into her lap.

With shaking hands, she pressed the screen and tried to scroll for Armand's name. She didn't know who else to call and could feel herself slipping away. She managed to bring his number into view and pressed dial. After two rings he picked up.

"Makayla?"

"Armand, help me."

CHAPTER ELEVEN

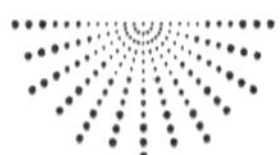

$\mathcal{A}$rmand nearly dropped his phone as he turned to Crone. "Kayla's in trouble." Before his brother could respond, he headed for the door. When he jumped in the car, Crone was already waiting for him. He squealed out of the garage and headed into the valley.

He ran his fingers through his hair. "Fuck!" Then slammed his fist into the steering wheel. "If not for Cyndel, I'd be there by now. Why can't I call my magic again?"

Crone tapped his fingers on his knee. "If not for Cyndel, you'd not be here at all."

This was true, and for a brief second he wondered what life would be like if he'd not met Kayla. The woman had touched something inside him and he wasn't sure yet how he felt about it.

He whipped into her driveway and they exited the car. Armand tried the front door.

"Fucking locked!"

Crone shoved him aside and touched the handle, unlocking then pushing it open. Armand ran inside.

"Kayla?" He saw what looked to be her computer in pieces on the floor and a busted chair in the kitchen. There had been a struggle.

Blood spotted the floor and cabinet. "Dear gods. Kayla?" His heart skipped several beats as he prayed to the gods and ran toward the bedroom. *Please let her be all right.*

When he entered the room with Crone on his heels, he heard a moan coming from the other side of the bed.

"Kayla!"

In a flash he was there and the sight of Kayla's broken and bruised body caused his blood to boil. He was down on the floor beside her in a second. He reached out to pull her into his arms.

"Wait," Crone yelled and knelt beside him. "Brother, she needs medical attention. I sense several broken ribs, a concussion. Damn, whoever did this meant business. She has internal injuries as well."

Armand clenched his fists and pulled back, afraid to cause her further pain. Instead he leaned in and brushed her forehead with a light kiss. It was then he realized he was falling in love with her. "*Querida,* who did this to you? I will find them and have them hanged."

"Armand," Kayla whispered through busted lips. She reached out to touch his hand. "It was the genie." Her head tipped to the side and he feared the worst. He touched her chest and felt the slight intake of air. Thank god she was still breathing, but for how much longer?

"Genie?" Crone asked.

"We only know one who would do this," Armand ground out through gritted teeth.

"Shit."

Armand gently kissed Kayla on the lips then stood. "Crone, you have to take her home to heal. It's the only place where Cyndel won't be able to reach her."

Crone reached out to touch her. "Agreed, but you know what this means?"

"It means I may not see her until you can return." He was releasing Kayla into the care of his brother. His heart shattered knowing it would be Crone who would care for her and not him. His eyes stung. "You will protect her as if she belonged to you."

Crone nodded. "With my life."

Armand watched as Crone turned to mist and disappeared with

Kayla. He'd been cursed to this earth for centuries, and yet he had never felt more alone then he did at this moment. He should be the one to care for her, be the first one her beautiful brown eyes gazed upon when she woke. He clenched his fists. "Cyndel! I command you to show yourself." His chest heaved with anger, but the room remained silent. "I swear to the gods, I will kill you with my bare hands."

KAYLA SLOWLY OPENED her eyes and looked through the haze that still clung to her. She wiggled her fingers and toes.

Still working.

Next she spread her arms and legs across a large mattress, they too appeared to be in working order. She pushed herself to sitting and it was then realization hit, she was not in a hospital. The burgundy quilt that covered her caught her eye with its gold swirling designs. She lifted her gaze to look across an expansive room between two large black oak pedestals on either side of the bed and took in the windows that lined the wall letting brilliant sunlight filter through the glass.

Someone cleared their throat and she glanced to the chair next to the bed. Intense blue eyes stared at her. She pulled the covers up to her chin.

"Who are you?"

He leaned forward. His black hair fell into his face. He looked menacing yet somehow familiar. He cocked a brow. "I am Crone. Armand's brother."

She blinked. Recognized the beautiful eyes. "So where is Armand? And where am I?"

He leaned back in the chair again and rubbed his goatee. "Well, you are a guest in my home and Armand ... that is a long story." He stood, tipped his head and studied her for a moment. "You'll find clothes in the closet that should fit. Take whatever you need. The bathroom is there." He pointed toward an open archway. "Once you've showered and dressed, meet me in the library. You should have no trouble finding your way around." He spun on his heel and left the room.

Kayla tossed off the covers and looked down at herself. She was wearing a mid-length red nightgown and her face heated at the thought of Crone seeing her naked. She also noted there were no bruises on her arms. She stretched out her legs, none there either. Swinging her feet to the plush carpet, she padded to the closet and was amazed there was no pain. She wondered how long she'd been here.

Flinging open the doors, she was astonished to see a room almost as big as where she stood. She stepped inside and found everything from shorts to dresses. The drawers had bras and panties in every color and her cheeks warmed looking at the lacy things and wondering if Armand would approve. She decided on jeans and a simple blouse then headed for the shower.

After a quick once over in the bathroom, she dressed and ran a comb through her hair. She wanted find out what was going on. Upon exiting the room, she found herself in a large airy hall. She looked to the right and saw a spiral oak staircase and figured it would lead the way.

Descending the marble stairs, she entered a grand hall and stared at the golden statues of men and women lining the wall and wondered who they were. She quickly passed through, skirted to the right, down a corridor with open archways and outside to an open terrace. Up ahead, she spotted Crone leaning against the doorjamb. He stepped aside to let her enter.

"Have a seat." He indicated a black leather couch in the center of a room full of books. They went from floor to ceiling and circled the entire room.

"Wow."

"Something to drink?"

"No, I'm good." She took a seat on the couch.

Crone sat across from her on an identical sofa. "Okay, I don't believe in pussy-footing around so I'll get right to it. You are no longer on earth, Armand and his entire family are Jinn and he was cursed by the genie that attacked you."

She blinked. "I kinda knew most of that."

He cocked a brow. "That brings me to the pendant you keep fondling. Where did you get it?"

She looked down at the heart shaped moonstone that hung around her neck, unaware she'd been rubbing it. "My great-grandmother."

"Do you know what it is?"

Kayla released the pendant, her wits finally coming back to her. "Wait, I should be asking you the questions. Why am I here and not in a hospital?"

Crone rolled his eyes. "Armand insisted you be brought here."

"Why?"

"I'll tell you in exchange for information on that pendant." His gaze fell between her breasts.

Did she trust him? After all, what did she really know about him or Armand? Nothing really. Yet what choice did she have? If what he said was true, and she was no longer on earth, then she had to rely on the man who sat in front of her. "Deal, but first I want to know how long I have been here. I only remember being beat up pretty bad." The memory of those violet eyes burning into her with such hatred caused her to shudder.

"You've been here for a week and yes, you had a few broken ribs and other cuts and bruises. Cyndel did a number on you. I made you a special tea to help you heal."

That explained why she felt so good. Not even a scab remained to indicate she'd been injured. "I guess I owe you my thanks. Still, why didn't you take me to a hospital?"

He leaned forward and steepled his fingers under his chin. "It would seem my brother has a thing for you. Now, enough of this and let me finish."

Crone went on to retell the tale that Armand had told earlier except he filled in a few of the blanks. Like how Armand was really a prince and in line to become ruler of his own house. That explained the power Cyndel had wanted. He also told how Armand had built the village and had to leave every generation before the people wondered why he never aged.

"So where does he go?" She understood he was confined to a limited area and was unable to travel past his barrier.

"He lives in a cave. Alone."

She let out a gasp.

"Mind you, I built it with all the comforts. However, he has to live there long enough for the elders to pass on and the new generation to not recognize him."

Kayla pursed her lip while her heart broke for him. She hated Cyndel even more.

"So let me see if I understand this correctly. Armand has no magic but remains immortal. He can't leave his confined area and you can only visit twice a year. Then at some point he has to dwell in a cave, alone."

The Jinn smiled. "You are very intelligent."

She crossed her arms over her breasts. "And you're an ass." She knew it was a stupid thing to say to a Jinn who had complete control over her life. Still, it was true.

He stared at her like she'd grown two heads then let out a barking laugh. "I can see why my brother likes you. You have spunk." He rose and walked to a table, picked up a silver bell and rang it. Immediately, two scantily clad women rushed into the room. Kayla watched, fascinated by their extreme beauty, as they set a tray of various fruits, a pitcher and two glasses on the table between the sofas. After they'd finished, they scurried away without a sound. Crone moved back to his seat opposite her and picked up a date.

"Help yourself."

"So, was that part of your harem?"

He arched a brow. "Perhaps. Now, on to the pendant. Tell me all you know."

With a sigh, she leaned over and grabbed a red grape. Crushing the fruit between her teeth she moaned at the burst of flavor in her mouth. She sensed the Jinn's impatience and somehow found it amusing.

"My nana gave it to me. Aren't you forgetting something very important?" Kayla wasn't sure why she felt the need to push the boundaries with this man. There was no doubt he could snuff out her life in a flash. Fear should be her friend, but she hadn't felt this exhilarated in years.

"I forget nothing. Continue," he demanded.

Squinting, she peered through slits. Why had Armand temporarily regained some of his powers? Crone didn't seem to want to speak about that fact and she would be damned if she'd let it go. However, she would placate the Jinn who sat across from her. "Anyway, she said it would protect me from evil. I only need to say the magical chant."

He leaned forward, his focus on her intent. "Do you remember the chant?"

She shook her head. "No. I was only a little girl."

His posture relaxed. "I see, and what does the chant do?"

She was done with their game of cat and mouse. "Something tells me you already know all there is about this pendant so why are you asking me?"

"Only to see what you know. I sense you tell the truth and don't remember. Whoever wears the pendant and chants the spell shall receive the power of the genie it is aimed at and … "

"Sending the genie to purgatory and giving the one who holds the pendant their power and immortality. I remember all that, just not the chant." She reached for a strawberry. "I never thought this stuff was real so I guess I didn't retain everything." She took a bite of the succulent fruit. "God, why is this stuff so much tastier here?"

"Because everything is better in our world. I would have thought fucking my brother would have proved that."

Kayla choked and went into a coughing fit. "My god, do you have no boundaries?" she replied after her air supply returned.

"None. Get used to it."

She'd had about enough of the Jinn's mouth and wanted to go home. There were a million questions she had for Armand. One being, where did this leave them and why did she even think there was a them? "When can I go home?"

"Not until we figure out how to keep you safe. Cyndel will kill you if you return to earth. Here—" He waved his hand through the air. "She can't touch you."

"But she didn't kill me and I need to see Armand."

He jumped from his seat and leaned over her, placing a hand on either side of her hip. She had no choice but to look up into his blue eyes. "Don't be foolish. I promised my brother I'd care for you as if you belonged to me. I will not break my vow. Are we clear?"

Care for her? Belonged to him? What the hell did it all mean? "Yes."

"Good." He straightened and moved back to his seat. "Now, I can only see one solution to this mess."

She swallowed, positive she wasn't going to like his answer. "And that is?"

"You have to use your pendant against Cyndel."

"I'm not going to have a choice am I? She wants me dead to keep me away from Armand."

Crone gave a hard smile. "It would seem there is something special about you that even Cyn has come to realize. You're the first she has ever tried to snuff out."

Kayla crossed her arms over her chest. "Great."

CHAPTER TWELVE

Kayla paced the library biting her nails. She stopped and turned to face Crone who stood on a ladder sorting through books. "This is insane! You're asking me to send a genie to purgatory and steal her power." She placed a hand on her hip. "Let's also not forget that I then become immortal!"

Crone cocked his head. "For the love of the gods, woman. Stop your fucking yapping and start searching."

"You really are an ass," she growled. Kayla walked to the other side of the room and stared at the wall of books. How the heck were they supposed to find the one that held the chant? Crone had said look for something old. They all looked ancient to her.

"Stupid Jinn," she mumbled.

"I heard that!"

"Good!" she shouted back. Her nerves were strung tight and she swore they were going to snap at any second. She reached up, pulled out a book and began thumbing through the pages then slammed it shut. "This one isn't even in a language I can read." Exasperated she pushed it back on the shelf.

"Need I remind you what's at stake?" he whispered in her ear.

Kayla jumped. "Damn it! Don't sneak up on me like that, and I know what's at stake."

"I'm not so sure. We are talking about my brother here. His family needs him."

Tears stung the back of her eyes. She understood, really she did. Crone had said Armand needed to take his place as king. War was brewing and they needed him here. Still, it was a lot to ask of her. What did she know of having magical powers? Not to mention immortality? What would she do? Where would she live? So many damn unanswered questions, not to mention the guilt. She shouldn't feel guilty for thinking of herself, but Armand had been cast out of his home and stranded for centuries. What must that be like? She couldn't even guess.

"Look." Crone's eyes softened. "I know we are asking you to change your entire life, but the only other choice you have is to stay here. Forever. Cyndel will kill you if you go back to earth."

She exhaled a deep breath. "Then I really have no choice. What if I fail?"

"Then Cyndel will probably kill you both."

"No pressure there." She raised her chin. "Maybe I will just stay here."

Crone laughed. "Go ahead. Do you think I'll make your life easy? No. You will be in my debt."

Kayla cringed. She could well imagine how miserable Crone could make her. There was one thing she'd learned in her brief time with this Jinn. He loved his brother and missed him terribly. She couldn't fault him for wanting to get Armand back home.

"Besides." He held a book up in front of her. "I have part of our answer."

"You found the chant?"

"No. But I now know why Armand gained some of his power and its even more reason for you to return with the amulet."

Kayla swallowed down her fear. "What is it?"

"You are his *vetemba*."

"His what?"

Crone strode toward the sofa with the old leather bound text in hand. "I should have realized it sooner, but never has a *vetemba* been human before." He sat and opened the worn pages.

Kayla sidled up next to him, her patience wearing thin. "You're going to have to explain." She looked at the pages and another language she couldn't read.

"It's a Jinn's other half. Usually the female comes in the form of another immortal and even then they are rare. We haven't seen one in over three thousand years."

"Wait. You mean there are other immortals?"

Crone snorted. "Of course. But I understand, you being human, it comes as a shock."

She dug her nails into her palm to keep from smacking him. "You really need to get over this human phobia of yours."

He nailed her with a glare. "I have no phobias." Then with a sigh. "I really don't mean any disrespect. It's simply in the scheme of things, humans are the weakest."

Well, she couldn't argue with him there, and for some stupid reason he was growing on her. Attitude and all. "I get it. So tell me more."

He flashed a cocky grin. "It would seem from what Armand has told me about how you were able to cool his fire, that you are his *vetemba*. His other half. If he were here, and at his full power, you would make him stronger. I surmise that since the curse removed his power you were able to somehow bring it back, if only partially."

She schooled her features to cover the hurt. Yet another thing Armand hadn't told her, and she couldn't help wonder what else he was hiding from her. Perhaps the only way to find out was through Crone. "Do you mean like how he was able to take away my chill?"

"Precisely. You draw from each other."

"So what exactly is the purpose of this other half?"

Crone slammed the book shut. "To procreate and strengthen the bloodline."

Kayla ground her teeth together. Her pulse beat in her temple. She plastered on a smile and batted her eyelashes. "Well then. This gives a whole new meaning to barefoot and pregnant." It sounded like a one-way street to her and one she would rather not go down. "So let's forget the *vetemba* part for a moment. What if I go back and I use the amulet. What happens if I succeed?"

"Meaning?"

"Oh, don't play stupid. Meaning, I'll be an immortal with powers I'll have no idea how to handle. What do I do with the rest of my so-called life?"

He shrugged. "That is between you and my brother, but I'm sure our father will see to it that you have a home here."

"Ah. The great Mr. Jinn. So when do I get the pleasure of meeting him?"

"How would now be?"

Kayla rose to face the deep voice that had spoken. There was no mistake, the man before her was their father. Same intense blue eyes, same dark hair but kept short. The man didn't look old enough to father sons who were thousands of years old.

He strode forward and extended his hand. "I am Efrain, Armand's father."

She extended her hand, which he grasped and brought to his lips. "I'm pleased to meet you." Her voice came out meeker than she'd have liked, but his power sent a surge of current up her arm causing bumps to rise.

"I must apologize for my son's actions." He glanced over at Crone who rolled his eyes. "He can be a bit overbearing at times, but he means well." He looped her arm around his and led her back to the sofas. "Crone, leave us."

Crone gave a slight bow. "As you wish." He made a quick exit from the room.

"Wow, he does have manners."

Efrain let out a hearty laugh. "He takes a bit of getting used to. I'm hoping his future wife will tame him."

Kayla snorted. "I feel sorry for her already."

He nodded. "Now. I know you must have questions. Please, feel free to ask me whatever you wish."

She decided right then and there she liked him. He made her feel at ease. "This is a big decision that you are all asking me to make. I mean I like Armand, don't get me wrong. It's just ... "

"I understand. Not only have you been sucked into a world you thought only a fairytale, but now you are being asked to change your very existence. Not to mention going up against Cyndel."

"Pretty much nailed it on the head." Mostly.

He patted her hand. "And all for a man you hardly know."

She could no longer hold back and the tears fell which ticked her off even more. She had no control over anything at the moment. "The thing is, Armand is the first man who actually seemed to care about my needs and how I felt, and now I find out he is not who I thought."

"Are you sure about that? I know I haven't had contact with my son in over a thousand years, and he made a mistake with Cyndel. He was young and naive and this mess is mostly my own fault, but he is a good man at heart," Efrain replied.

Kayla wiped her eyes. "How is this your fault?"

"I knew Cyndel was using him for power and wealth. I'd hoped she would cure Armand of his womanizing. I never expected she was capable of cursing him. I though the worst would be he'd end up with a broken heart and learn a lesson."

"Oh, I see."

"You must think I'm a terrible father."

She met his gaze. "Who am I to judge? I never told anyone that I knew, months before I confronted my ex-husband, that he was cheating. I'd hoped he would come to his senses." She shook her head. "I was so stupid. He had the best of both worlds, why would he give it up?"

His features softened. "We all make mistakes. It's only when we don't learn from them that we deserve whatever fate hands us. I can't ask you to sacrifice for my family, it's a choice only you can make. I will tell you that you have a home here and I will help you in any way I can."

Kayla was deeply touched. Granted, he wanted his son back, but she sensed he was sincere. "Thank you. I really appreciate it."

"Also for what's its worth, I believe Armand cares for you or he wouldn't have insisted Crone bring you here." He gave her a warm smile. "As for the *vetemba*. Don't take what Crone says to heart. Being Armand's other half is much more than bringing him power or children. It's a love and sharing like no other and it's a bit hard to explain. It has to be experienced."

There was so much to consider her head pounded. What would happen between her and Armand should she decide to save him? Did they have a future together? Did she want one? In her heart she knew she loved him, but discovering he was a prince and soon to be king made her wonder if she expected too much from him.

"Tell me. Do Armand and I have a choice as far as being together?"

Efrain closed his eyes and took a deep breath before looking at her. "Yes. Either of you can choose to walk away. There have been cases of the *vetemba* and the Jinn not falling in love and therefore not making a good match. Usually the female will find a more suitable match."

Great. I can love him but not necessarily the other way around.

"I have also discovered how your grandmother came to possess the amulet."

Excitement zinged through her. "Really? How? I mean how did you find out and how did she get it?" Finally, part of this mystery would be solved.

"I went through some very old scrolls that are kept in my personal archive. I must admit I'm very excited that you came into our lives. Your great-grandmother, Ilsa, was once a Jinn."

Her jaw dropped. "I don't … I mean. How can that be?" She had not expected to hear those words at all. It had occurred to her Nana had somehow had contact with the immortals, but this?

"Let me start from the beginning." Efrain rubbed his jaw. "Your family were the real rulers of the House of Unaria: the house that Cyndel's father now rules. Ilsa was also a *vetemba*, and Alistair, who was Cyndel's great grandfather, fell in love with Ilsa. However, she refused him for she had fallen in love with a mortal."

"Great-grandpa?"

He nodded. "That would be my guess. The story goes she feared Alistair, and as it turned out had good reason. He had a curse placed on her and turned her mortal."

Kayla could only stare at Efrain in disbelief. No words would form.

"This, of course, created a war between the families. In the end, your ancestors were slaughtered by Alistair and your house overtaken."

She rubbed her forehead. "Oh my god. This is simply too much to believe."

He sighed. "I'm afraid there is more. Ilsa still had friends in the Jinn community and someone, though we still don't know who, made her the amulet. It was meant to protect her children and it worked until your parents' death."

Her bottom lip trembled and tears formed. "The plane crash. They were on their way to England. I was only three when they died."

He touched her hand. "I'm so sorry. It is suspected that Alistair had a hand in their death. I'm going to guess that Cyndel is aware of who you are, and that is the real reason she wants you dead. You are the rightful heir to the House of Unaria. The amulet is meant not only to protect you, but bring back your family's power."

She was stunned. So many emotions raced through her. Sadness for the family she had lost. Anger at the ones who stole their lives.

Efrain brushed a tear from her cheek. "I'm afraid this really leaves you with no choice."

She pulled back her shoulders and shoved the pity deep into the back of her mind. "They took those I love. I have no idea what I'm doing, but I guess we better find that chant. I have a genie to fight." Even if Armand abandoned her, she couldn't let him suffer any longer and she owed her family.

Efrain slid off the couch to his knees, his head bowed. "I will be forever in your debt. You will also have the alliance of the House of Reviana."

She was horrified. "Oh don't." She reached to touch his shoulder. "Please, get up. You shouldn't be kneeling."

He winked at her and pushed himself back to his feet. "You should get used to it. Your station in this world dictates it." He held out his hand to help her up. "Besides, it also means Crone would have to drop to his knees in your presence." He let out a hearty laugh and she couldn't help but join in.

"I really do like you."

He gave her a big grin. "The feeling is mutual. Come, let me show you what awaits you."

He led her through an open set of French doors and onto a balcony. He pointed to a vast body of water where turquois waves crashed onto a snow-white sandy beach. "The mountains you see on the horizon. They belong to you. The House of Unaria rests in the valley, as do your people."

She swallowed the lump in her throat. So many people were counting on her to succeed.

ARMAND HADN'T SLEPT in weeks. Not since Crone had left with Kayla's broken body. Since he was unable to have contact with his family, he had no idea if she was even still alive. Cyndel had made sure that the curse even covered modern day technology. Guilt racked him. If not for him, Kayla would never have been hurt. He prayed every day for her recovery.

He paced the kitchen not knowing what to do with himself. He tried calling Cyndel, but she continued to ignore his summons. He still didn't understand why she had attacked Kayla. He'd slept with other woman, hundreds of them during his time on earth, and never had she harmed them. So what was different this time? The only conclusion was that Kayla had returned his magic.

A knock interrupted his thoughts. He jerked his head up and glared at the door. It was eleven at night, who the hell would be banging at this hour? With the stealth of a cat, he eased to the front of the house. The porch light had come on so he looked through the peephole. In seconds, he unbolted the locks and flung open the door.

"By the gods, you're all right." He grabbed Kayla by the hand and pulled her past the entryway and into his arms. He touched his nose to her hair and inhaled her scent. Nothing in his entire existence ever felt as good as she did pressed against him. He leaned back and looked down into her eyes. "*Querida,* I have been worried sick about you. I tried not to fear the worst, but it was impossible."

She flashed that warm smile he loved so much. "I'm so sorry. I wish I could have gotten word to you sooner. There just wasn't any way."

He shook his head. "No. It's I who should apologize. It's because of me that you were hurt in the first place." He peered over her head as if expecting to see his enemies outside, then pulled her the rest of the way into the house and shut the door.

"How is it that you're here? It's not time for Crone to come back yet. It has only been–"

"Three weeks. I hounded him to bring me home until he couldn't stand my nagging. He dropped me off as close as he could get and I took a bus the rest of the way." She placed her palm on his cheek. "I needed to let you know I was okay."

He released her and paced again. "You could have called me instead of coming here. I would have packed your things for you and shipped them to any address of your choosing." He stopped. "It is not safe here. You must leave."

"I'm not safe anywhere, Armand. At least, not according to your brother and father. They tell me Cyndel will come after me no matter where I go."

"No. I will negotiate your safety. If you promise to leave and never come back, I believe I can get her to leave you alone." If he could only get the genie to answer his call, he was sure he could get her to agree.

"Has she been back since I left?"

"No. She ignores me."

"Then how can you guarantee my safety?"

I will make the ultimate sacrifice. I will marry Cyndel. "I need you to trust me. I know I'm asking a lot of you, but please."

She crossed her arms over her breasts. Breasts he wanted so badly to release from their confinement and shower with affection. He wanted to declare his feelings, but it would benefit no one.

"Well, truth is, I'm here to save my ass and break your curse."

"Excuse me?"

She reached for a chain around her neck and pulled it out from under her tee.

He ground his teeth. "Where did you get that?" This had to be a sick joke. No way in hell did she have a real amulet. It was a Jinn fable read to the children at bedtime. No one, not even the elders, had ever seen one and certainly no one believed they really existed.

"Long story short, my nana gave it to me." She moved to the couch and took a seat. Worry wore on her face and he hated the fact he'd put it there.

"You think you're going to use that against Cyndel?" He stood there gaping at her, not knowing what else to do. He couldn't get too close to her again or he'd have her undressed and beneath him screaming his name. Damn, he needed her.

"Between Crone, Efrain and myself we managed to find the text with the chant. It took us four days of tossing books to find that damn thing." She leaned back and pinched the bridge of her nose.

"No. I forbid this."

She looked over at him like he was insane. "Well, your father needs you to come home and I'm not ready to die at the hands of some crazed bitch."

He couldn't stand it anymore. He moved to sit next to her and took her hand in his. Somehow he had to make her understand. "You're no match for her and I am powerless to help. If she were to show up right now, I could do nothing. I've tried to no avail to call my power again." He stared at the pendant. "There is no guarantee this will work. I'm sure my father told you that."

She flicked out her tongue and moistened her lips. *Do not kiss her.* She had to believe there was nothing between them. It was the only way to save her.

"Yes, but he was confident it would if done correctly. What about the fact that I am your *vetemba*?"

"That's not possible," he whispered. Yet he knew he lied. After she had left, he realized what she was and that made his decision even more difficult. Her safety, however, was more important than anything else. "Even if you were, it is apparent to me that we are not a match."

He watched her bite her lip and knew the words had stung. He needed to keep up his attack and make her hate him. "Let us say you succeeded in killing Cyndel. Then what? You will have lost your mortality and gained who knows what kind of power. You will be clueless on how to handle it. Where will you go?"

"Your father promised to help me."

He tossed his head back and laughed. "I don't think you fully understand the ramifications of your actions. You will never see your family and friends again. Humans can never know we exist."

"I have no family and while I love my friend, Nikki ... I understand."

"You cannot forfeit your life. Stay here and find a man who will love you and be happy. Raise your children together, grow old and watch your grandchildren be born." He couldn't miss the hurt in her eyes and it was killing him, but he couldn't stop now. "You didn't think that you and I ... ? I mean we had fun, but that's all it was." He schooled his features. "I could never love a human. It is beneath me."

She looked away. "What about you and the curse. Don't you want to go home?"

Even after he just dealt her that blow, she was still thinking of him. He closed his eyes and inhaled. Time to twist the knife. "I'm going to marry Cyndel and all this will end."

She whipped her head around, her eyes wide. "I thought you hated her? From what your family said, she tricked you. Why would you marry her?"

"I can think of several reasons. One, I'm tired of being stuck here, and as you say, my family needs me. Two, I need a queen. Cyndel will not only fill the role but also provide me with strong sons. It's also the right thing to do. Just as putting you on a bus to the airport, first thing in the morning, is also the right thing to do. You will rest here tonight, then at day break we will gather your things and get you out of here."

She looked away. "I see. You're right, of course. It's probably for the best, but I still don't understand how marrying her will keep her from killing me later. You're giving her everything she wants so there will be nothing to stop her."

Why the hell couldn't things be simple for once in his fucking life? Sure he screwed up, but how long should he be held accountable? He'd done so many good things since then, giving back to his small part of this world. He jumped up from his seat next to Kayla before he forgot all common sense and took her right there.

"Just believe I have my ways to guarantee your safety." He really didn't have a plan, but if he had to marry Cyndel then keep her locked up to protect Kayla, then that's exactly what he'd do.

CHAPTER THIRTEEN

Makayla tossed and turned lying in the same bed she and Armand had slept in not long ago. Fury stirred in her that he would put her up in his room. A house of this size had to have guest rooms, but he'd insisted and against her better judgment she'd stayed. Part of her hoped he would change his mind. She also knew that Cyndel would come looking for her no matter what. She chose to keep the information she'd learned about her family to herself. She had wanted to tell Armand, but she also needed him to desire her for who he thought she was and not who she could become.

She'd learned that if her and Armand were to marry, their houses would join and make both of them very powerful. She had to know he loved her for all the right reasons. Either way she had decided to fight Cyndel and take back what belonged to her.

She sensed Armand lingered just outside the door, guarding her, listening for any sign of distress. Trouble was, he had caused her current discomfort. She didn't know what to expect when she came back. The look of relief on his face, when he had greeted her at the door and pulled her into his arms, would make one think he cared about her in a way a husband cares for his wife. But she had been dead wrong.

She punched her pillow wishing it were his head. In reality, it wasn't his fault. She knew when she'd slept with him it was only a fling, a good time. But tell that to her heart. Somehow, he'd broken past the barrier she'd held in place to keep others from hurting her and showed her how to live again. Now she remembered why she'd stayed out of relationships, she always ended up broken.

"Why can't I simply use a guy for sex without my heart getting in the damn way?" It was going to be a long, sleepless night. Tomorrow she had no doubt her life would change drastically.

For now, she'd lie in Armand's bed, take in his scent for the last time and try not to remember what it felt like to be his. To feel his lips pressed against her breasts, her thighs, her ....

"Damn it!" Kayla threw back the covers and leapt from the bed. Her heart raced and her sex ached. She needed air so she headed for the door and flung it open, intent on going to the patio. She walked right into strong, muscular flesh.

He stood in her way wearing only a pair of faded jeans. She stared at his naked chest then dragged her gaze upward until she met his eyes. Sapphire blue, filled with heat, stared back at her. He'd tied his hair back, only adding to his rugged look.

She whimpered.

He grabbed her by the arms and walked her backwards until the back of her legs hit the bed. When she could go no further, he kissed her. Hard. Desperate. Not what you'd give a woman who meant nothing to you.

Her body responded. Need spread like wildfire through her, and she was beyond caring about anything except the moment and how badly she wanted him.

He pushed her back on the bed, his body covering her. He grabbed the neckline of her tee and ripped it open, exposing her nakedness underneath. Hot lips latched onto a nipple and she arched into him. She touched his biceps and the strength beneath her fingertips heated her core.

When he moved his attention to the other nipple, he jerked her shorts off and slid two fingers through her folds and into her sex.

She moaned. Her desire for him was going to make her combust. "I need you," she whispered.

He pulled his fingers free and locked onto her gaze while he pulled off his jeans. The tip of his cock pressed into her then slid home. His eyes never left hers as he shifted his hips and moved in and out. He was looking into her soul, searching for something.

She clawed at his back and met each thrust, unable to get enough of him. Still his gaze never wavered until his lips crashed against hers. He kissed her with a hunger she'd never felt before and her heart shattered. She wanted this moment to last forever, but something inside warned he was saying goodbye. One last moment of rapture before they parted ways.

Her orgasm started deep, as a slow spark, then grew until she was pulling the sheets between her fingers. Her breath caught as her whole body went flush from the heat. Never had an orgasm been so intense. She rode the roller coaster, cresting at the top then spiraling downward with no ending in sight until Armand broke the kiss. He arched his back, his own orgasm filling her.

"*Te amo, querida.*" He pulled her close to him and nuzzled her neck. Their heartbeats synced in rhythm. "You should have stopped me."

"I didn't want to," she whispered. She rubbed his back. "What did you say to me a minute ago?"

His body stiffened. He pulled free from her, rolled off and lay next to her. "It's not important. This changes nothing between us, Kayla."

Why did she feel like he was lying to her? She propped herself up on one elbow. "Tell me the truth. You don't really want to marry Cyndel, do you?"

"That is irrelevant. It is what it is and you cannot change it."

He refused to meet her gaze and she felt her ire stirring again. She sat up and moved on top of him so he had to look at her. "Bullshit. You can't tell me that this meant nothing to you. That I mean nothing to you." She stared him down, waiting for his response.

His eyes went dark and cold. "I care that you are safe as I would for any other living creature. Stop reading more into this." He pushed her away and jumped to his feet. Grabbing his jeans from the floor, he slipped them on. "You will be leaving in a few hours. I suggest you rest." He was gone, leaving her alone again.

She grabbed a pillow and threw it at the door. Somehow she had to reach him and stop this madness. She could not let him marry Cyndel to save her. She rehashed the conversation with Efrain and formed a plan.

MORNING CAME and Kayla hadn't slept a wink, but she had a plan. She sat across from Armand at the kitchen table and played with her food. "Armand, you can't marry Cyndel."

He looked up from his plate. "Are we back to this again? Why can you not let it go?"

She put down her fork, set her shoulders and looked him square in the eyes. "Because I love you." She knew she was setting herself up for a broken heart, but he had to know how she felt. Maybe it would be enough to get through to him. She realized she could tell him who she actually was and it would probably change everything. However, she needed him to love her and right now she dared not trust her gut. She had to be positive how he really felt.

"You are a foolish woman. Save your heart for someone who cares."

She refused to back down. "Besides, how do you intend to make me leave?"

Tossing his napkin on the table as if it were a challenge, he rose from his seat, stalked around to the other side, picked her up out of the chair and tossed her over his shoulder. She pummeled his back.

"What the hell are you doing? Put me down," she demanded.

"Teaching you to respect my authority," he growled.

Armand tossed her into the car and strapped her in. Before she could free herself, he was in the driver's seat and had the vehicle backing out of the garage.

"Are you really going to go through with this?" Anger knifed through her and she smacked him on the arm. He didn't flinch.

"You leave me no choice."

He ranted something under his breath in Spanish and she was sure she didn't want a translation. Could she have been wrong about him? She stared out the window as they drove up the mountain rather than into town.

"I thought you were taking me to the bus depot?"

"Change of plans. There is a small airstrip on the other side of the mountain. I have friends there that will fly you to the main airport." He glared at her. "You have proven to me you cannot be trusted to behave."

This time she punched him in the arm. "You're an ass just like your brother. I'm not a damn child."

His nostrils flared. "Did my brother harm you?"

Seriously? She crossed her arms over her chest and looked out the window. Did he forget she knew how to read body language? At the moment, his indicated he was pissed. "What if he had? Why would you care?"

The car came to a screeching halt and had it not been for the seatbelt, she would have hit the dash. When she looked over at him, his lip was curled into a snarl. *So the lion has woken. Imagine that. And yet he says he doesn't care.*

"Don't play games with me, *querida*. It does not bode well for either of us," he replied through clenched teeth.

"Really? It would seem you are a master at it, pretending you don't give a shit about me. I don't believe you, Armand. This little fit of yours just proved you're a liar."

His jaw went stiff and he focused on the road. He slammed the shifter into gear and proceeded down the mountain. They drove in silence and she smiled knowing she'd struck a nerve. Now she needed to figure out how to keep from getting on that plane. Could he really make her? He had overpowered her once and she had no idea what to expect from his so-called friends. If she was forced to fly from here, then she needed a plan B to get herself back.

"I give up, Armand. I will go home willingly." She watched his body relax. Good, he'd taken the bait, but what next? Two large buildings and an airstrip came into view. *Shit.* They were here.

He pulled the car inside one of the hangers and shut off the ignition. He exited and came around to open her door. She undid her belt and accepted his hand while trying not to think of what his touch did to her.

"Seems awfully quiet in here," she stated.

"We were not expected for another hour so we will have to wait."

She nodded. "I see." She walked to the edge of the hanger and looked out over the mountainous terrain. "So how far from home are you allowed to go?"

He moved in beside her. "This is it. You see that tree over there?" He pointed toward a field on the other side of the runway. "I can't walk to it. The other side of this strip is off limits."

"Really? What happens if you try?" A plan formed in her head. She needed to get him to the edge of his boundary.

He shrugged. "It's like walking into a wall. I simply can't cross it."

"Fascinating. Can you show me?"

"Why?" His eyes narrowed.

Kayla tried to keep her features schooled, not wanting him to become too suspicious. "I simply can't fathom how this magic works." She shrugged and acted nonchalant. "Besides, what else do we have to do while we wait?"

"Very well." He grabbed her hand and escorted her across the runway. The morning sun was just beginning its climb into the sky, and the air still held its crispness from the previous night. He stopped at the edge of the pavement and pressed his palms into the air. "I can't cross here."

She stepped off the edge of the runway. "You mean you can't touch me now?"

"No, now come back over here," he demanded.

"If you can't touch me then you can't make me." She was feeling pretty proud of herself for having tricked him. Trouble was, now what? She had to flee before his friends arrived, but first she needed to know. "Tell me what you said to me after making love last night?"

He paced. "We didn't make love. I fucked you and that is all. Now get back over here."

A light bulb went off inside her head. "God, how stupid." She pulled her phone from her back pocket and began scrolling for the translator. She hesitated. Did she really want to know? What if the words were not what she hoped for? She swallowed her fear and pressed the screen. "*Te Amo, querida.*"

"I love you, darling." The monotone voice replied back.

CHAPTER FOURTEEN

rmand listened as Kayla's phone spoke the words he should have never said to her. How the hell was he going to get out of this mess? "It was the heat of the moment. It meant nothing."

She stepped closer, but still out of reach. "I love you, Armand."

He dropped his gaze to the ground. "Don't."

"Armand, look at me," she begged.

His gaze drifted to her warm brown eyes and what he saw there was raw and real. "Damn it. You can't love me."

"Why?"

"Because I can't stand the thought of watching your death." She tipped her head in confusion. He didn't expect her to understand.

"You mean my growing old and you staying immortal? All the more reason to end this curse."

"No, you will not sacrifice for me. I cannot allow it." He stood steadfast, prepared to argue with her when a glint behind her caught his eye. "Kayla, get behind me. Now!"

Rather than obey him, she spun around to look behind her.

"How lucky for me that I should find both of you here?" Cyndel hissed.

"Cyndel. You will leave the girl alone." Armand fisted his hands and wondered how the hell he would protect Kayla. "I will marry you, but you must agree to leave the girl in peace." Those words cut through him like hot steel. He despised the thought of marrying her, but would do anything to protect Kayla. Even die for her.

Cyndel circled Kayla like a predator does its prey. "Oh, I don't want to marry you. I'm centuries past that." She curled her lip into a snarl. "With you gone, little human, I'll no longer have to worry. You are the last of the line."

"What are you talking about? Why are you doing this? Why have you not released me from my prison?" He tried again to cross the threshold, hoping she'd broken the spell, but the wall held firm.

She flashed violet eyes at him. "Because it suits me to torture the human. Even better that I can make you watch while I slowly kill her. When I'm done with her, I will kill you next."

Panic gripped his heart and squeezed. He was helpless to save the woman he loved. "Cyndel, kill me if you want. Torture me for the next century if it pleases you, but let the girl go." He dropped to his knees. "I am begging you."

Cyndel tapped her finger against her lips. "Hmm. Now I'm not sure which would prove more entertaining. Making you watch her death, or having her watch yours."

He gritted his teeth. "If you no longer care for me, then why must you harm the girl?" He was afraid he already knew the answer. The fire behind the genie's eyes indicated she'd finally gone mad. His Jinn screeched within him, demanding release to protect what belonged to him, but wasn't going to happen. For the first time since Kayla had returned, he wished her to use the amulet. The moonstone she wore around her neck might be the only thing that could save her. He had to keep Cyndel distracted and pray Kayla would use the opportunity to her advantage. He just hoped his next move didn't provoke the genie to lash out on Kayla.

Armand rose to his feet and moved in close to the barrier. "Cyndel, you want to know the real reason I didn't marry you?" He prayed her vanity would be her undoing.

"Humor me, I have all day," Cyndel replied, inspecting her nails with boredom.

"You were a rotten fuck. I only pretended to enjoy your company." It was enough to elicit sparks from her fingertips.

"In this stone I behold, powers of which shall not be told," Kayla yelled.

"That's right!" Armand yelled louder. Kayla had started the chant and he needed to keep the she bitch occupied. "How's your ego now, Cyndel. Even your own army thought you worthless in bed." He watched her ire grow.

"Where it once held ice, it now holds fire. Containing the cursed and their desire."

Cyndel screeched and spun to face Kayla. "You bitch!" She shot a blast of power aimed at Kayla's chest sending her flying.

SEARING pain shot through Kayla's chest at the same time she heard Armand yell her name. She landed with a hard thud several feet away, the air knocked from her lungs. With no idea where the genie was, she knew she had to regain herself and finish the chant before they both died. She rolled to her side.

"To turn the fire back to ice. Kiss the fire, kiss it thrice." She brought the stone to her lips. Once. Twice.

A second blast hit her back causing a blood-curdling scream to escape her lips.

"Kayla!" Armand yelled.

"You think you can destroy me? Human?" Cyndel laughed. "You will never succeed. You are a fool just as your forefathers before you."

The hair on Kayla's arms rose and wafted in the breeze. She heard Armand shouting, but was unable to make out what he said. Pain shot through her body and stars danced before her eyes. *Keep it together. You have to fight back.* She focused on the two things most important to her: Armand and retribution.

She kissed the stone a third time. "With this blessed kiss of three …
"

Another shot and Kayla was flung into the air. Landing on her arm, she heard bone shatter. Blood ran from her mouth, but her gaze met Armand's who knelt a few feet away and his tear stained face made her more determined to live. "The genie's heart of ice shall not be free."

Armand tipped his head back and yelled to the heavens. Black smoke wafted around him in a slow dance then tightened and transformed into a funnel that reached several feet into the air. The winds whipped and debris flew past. She cried out as her body skidded over the rough terrain.

As suddenly as it started, all fell quiet. Kayla lay on her back staring at a blue sky. The birds chirped their daily song as if nothing had ever happened. She tried to sit up, but her broken body refused to move. She turned her head to where Armand had been.

Gone.

She tried to look around for Cyndel, but didn't see her. Had she succeeded? "Armand?"

Only the birds answered back.

"Dear god, what have I done?" Tears flowed as the racking sobs overtook her. Had she sent him to purgatory as well? Maybe the amulet couldn't discern between Armand and Cyndel. Why the hell had she not thought of that? Why had Crone or Efrain not told her? They must not have known, otherwise they would never have risked Armand's life. What the hell was she going to do now? Her broken body was useless and black spots danced in front of her. She could do nothing but lie there and remember to breathe.

15

CHAPTER FIFTEEN

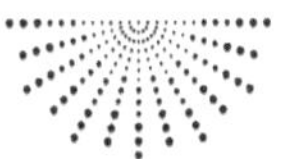

$\mathcal{A}$rmand was careful as he picked up Kayla's broken body and brought her close to his chest. He kissed her lips and shared his power with her own to speed the healing process. Pride swelled in his chest at how his little vixen had stood up to a powerful genie. He also remembered the fear that ate him raw as he watched her get tossed like a rag doll. Later, he would reprimand her for being so careless with her life. Never had he thought someone besides his father and brothers could mean more to him, but with his mate tucked close to him he vowed he would never let her go.

He flashed them to his bedroom and was greeted by Crone, Lazaro and his father as he laid her on the bed.

"Is she well?" Efrain asked.

Armand nodded. "Her broken bones are already mending. I expect she will be fully recovered by morning."

Lazaro stepped forward. "I have missed you, brother."

Armand pulled his brother into an embrace. "I have missed you as well." Emotions overwhelmed him as he clung to a man who had only been a boy when last he saw him. He pushed back. "You have grown."

Lazaro laughed. "Yes, I have. We have many things to catch up on but after your mate recovers."

103

Armand nodded. "Thank you."

Efrain approached. His eyes watered. "I cannot even begin to tell you how much I have missed you. I am sorry I didn't protect you from Cyndel."

Armand pulled his father into him. "Don't. I was the only one responsible for my actions." He released his father and bent to one knee. "I beg your forgiveness, my king."

His father palmed his cheek. "You were forgiven long ago. Take care of *your vetemba* and come to me when you are ready."

Armand nodded and watched his family disappear. He rose and walked back to Kayla's side, deciding this was not the place he wanted her to awaken. He had a special place in mind. He curled in next to her and whispered the magical words that transported them to his bungalow. He would not leave their bed until she awoke.

His mind moved back to the events earlier in the day. When Kayla had completed the chant, all hell had broken loose. Armand's power and that of Cyndel's had created a strong vortex as it whipped in the atmosphere and searched for its host. Armand's Jinn had awakened fully and welcomed its power back. When the energy reentered his body, it had been more than he could consume and sent him into his smoke form. It had been all he could do to fight it and return back to Kayla. He had no idea what had happened to her in the short time he was gone.

Lying next to her, he sensed her power awakening. She was immortal and on the mend, but it was a good thing she slept. Broken bones knitting back together was painful no matter who you were. He kissed her cheek. "*Te amo, querida.* Sleep well my little angel."

MAKAYLA OPENED her eyes and stared at the ceiling fan that whooshed in slow motion. Checking the function of her body parts when she woke was becoming way too familiar of a routine. She sensed someone beside her and slowly turned her head, not sure what to expect. However, meeting the intense blue gaze she had grown so fond of warmed her insides.

"You are awake," Armand whispered.

"You're okay?"

He propped up on one elbow. "I am perfect, thanks to you."

She looked around and found herself in a large open room and she swore she heard waves crashing outside. "Where are we?"

"My private tropical isle."

She sat up. "Seriously?" It was then she realized she was naked. "Uh, where are my clothes?"

He snorted. "You're worried about what you're wearing?"

She pulled the sheet to cover her breasts. "Well last I remember, I was half dead in the middle of nowhere and you vanished in a puff of smoke. I thought I'd sent you with Cyndel." She gasped. "She is gone, right? You … you have your powers back?"

He nodded. "Yes to both questions."

"So I'm guessing I'm now immortal?"

His lip curled into a most wicked grin ever. "Very and all healed."

She narrowed her gaze. "Why are you looking at me like that? Did I grow two heads or something?" She reached up and touched her hair just to be sure.

"No, you still have one. For now."

"What?" Panic set in. No one ever really told her what would happen when she took Cyndel's power. *Great. Now I'm a freak.*

He rolled into a thunderous laughter. "I kid."

She pursed her lips. "I'm not finding the entertainment value here."

He sat up and it was then she noticed he was buck-naked. *How the hell did I miss that?* He looked different, but she couldn't place it exactly. It must have shown on her face.

"*Querida,* now you look at me as if I have two heads."

"Something's different about you."

He smiled. "You are most observant."

She turned away, afraid to face him. Her fingers itched to trace the hardened muscles of his chest, down his abs and wrap around his …

She rubbed her palm over her face. *Dear god,* she had to figure out how to get out of bed and get some clothes.

"I can hear your thoughts and I like you better naked."

She whipped her gaze back at him. "What?"

He shrugged. "You are Jinn, we can read each other's thoughts."

"No! How the hell do I turn it off?" This wasn't good. Not at all. Having him know her every thought– "Wait, then why can't I hear yours?"

"You will in time, when you become more practiced. You'll also learn how to block others from yours. There are many things I have to teach you, but before I do … " He sprang at her. Pinning her body to the bed, he held her arms over her head and brushed a kiss across her lips. "I find the need to bury myself deep inside you."

She shivered. So many things had happened between them. Words had passed, but where did it leave them? Did they have a future? It was hard to think straight with him peppering kisses along her neck. He leaned back and eyes filled with desire bore into her and touched her soul.

"I meant the words I whispered to you. Never before has a woman affected me in such a manner."

"Then why were you willing to marry Cyndel?" She knew but needed to hear the words pass his lips.

"I would do anything to protect you. Including live an eternal hell with a witch like her. When she attacked you and I could do nothing but watch, I nearly died."

She understood, really she did. When Cyndel threatened his life, it scared her more than anything ever had. "But you knew I had the pendant and the ability to stop her and give you your life back."

"I could not take a chance that it would work. It wasn't that I didn't believe in you. I didn't want to gamble with your life." He kissed her. Deep, passionate and tender. When he broke away, they were both breathless. "I love you and I want you to be mine for eternity."

She gasped. "Armand, what are you saying?"

"Become my queen, *querida.* Marry me."

She wiggled beneath him and tried to free her arms. "Armand, let me loose. I need to touch you."

He obliged and she put her arms around his neck and pulled him into her. "I love you and I'd like nothing more than to be yours. Forever."

Their lips fused and tongues tangled in a slow exotic dance. Armand tasted of sex and spice and she couldn't get enough.

He broke off, suckled her neck then moved to her breast and ran his tongue around the edge of her nipple, making her dig her nails into his back. A strange sensation of floating came over her and she spotted the sun high in the sky.

Her heart sped up. "Armand, what the hell?" They floated on a large raft in the middle of a deep blue sea.

"Have you ever made love in the middle of the ocean before?" he whispered.

"No, I haven't."

"Relax and enjoy the ride." He lifted his gaze. "We are capable of many things. Trust me to care for you."

She relaxed. She trusted him with every fiber of her being and would enjoy everything he had to offer.

He sucked her nipple, swirled and nipped before moving to the other. His fingers slid between her apex and pressed inside.

She arched to meet him. "So good, but I don't want to wait. I need you in me. Now." A little voice in the back of her mind said she had to tell him the truth. *Later.*

Armand wrapped his arms under her thighs, spread her legs and entered her in one thrust.

She moaned.

He stayed buried and brought his lips to her ear. "Are you all right?

"More than all right, but sex in the middle of the ocean will take some getting used to." She had the feeling there would be a lot of things she'd have to get used to. The biggest would be waking up next to this man everyday for eternity. She couldn't wait to start their new life.

Armand slid his cock out, then back in. His pace increased causing her muscles to clench and heat flooded her core. Kayla rode a tidal wave of pleasure so intense she wasn't sure she'd survive. She thought her last orgasm with Armand had been earthshattering. She floated to another plane of existence and back again. Aftershocks of mini-orgasms rolled through her until Armand roared, his own release causing another tidal wave of intense pleasure to wash over her.

When her breathing finally returned to normal, she realized they were back in bed. "Dear god that was … I have no words to even describe it."

"Everything is better as a Jinn. You will get used to it," he replied.

"I'm not sure I want to. I mean, I've never had sex this great. I have to admit even the way you travel is pretty freaking awesome."

Armand pulled free and rolled to his back, pulling her to sit on top of him. "I will make sure you never want or need for anything, *querida*. You deserve only the best." He opened his hand. "And I will start with this." He placed a brilliant ruby on her left ring finger.

"Where were you hiding this? It's absolutely beautiful." She bent down and brushed a kiss on his lips. "I love you, Armand."

He chuckled. "I called it forth from my home in Reviana. It's been in safe keeping waiting for someone special." He cupped her face. "I can't wait to take you to see my world … our new home."

She pulled in a breath. "There is something you should know." She relayed the entire story about Cyndel's family and how her nana had come to have the amulet. His eyes grew wide.

"Why did you not tell me this before?"

"Please don't be angry with me." She licked her lips. "I needed to know you loved me and wanted me and not my kingdom." She waited, holding her breath.

He burst out in laughter. "I understand and I don't care if you have a thousand kingdoms or a condo in Chicago. I love you."

She let her breath escape. "What happens now?"

He pulled her closer. Kissed the tip of her nose. "I won't lie, there will be war. Cyndel's remaining family is strong, but you have the backing of the House of Reviana and I'm certain others will follow once they learn the truth."

"I understand. As long as I have you, I can get through anything."

"I will always walk beside you."

"I need to talk to Nikki, she'll be frantic if I vanish from the face of the planet." She cocked her head. "What about your village and the people there? They rely on you."

He brushed a kiss across her lips eliciting a moan. "You do what you think is best with your friend. If you feel you can trust her to keep our secrets, then I don't see why you have to sever your relationship completely. She'll always be welcome in our home. As far as the village, we'll be back and my people will always be taken care of."

Tears ran down her cheeks. She was closing one chapter of her life and opening another. She couldn't have written a happier ending herself.

ABOUT THE AUTHOR

Award winning and bestselling author Valerie Twombly grew up watching Dark Shadows over her mother's shoulder, and from there her love of the fanged creatures blossomed. Today, Valerie has decided to take her darker, sensual side and put it to paper. When she is not busy creating a world full of steamy, hot men and strong, seductive women, she juggles her time between a full-time job, hubby and her two German shepherd dogs, in Northern IL. Valerie is a member of Romance Writers of America and Fantasy, Futuristic and Paranormal Romance Writers. She is also the founder of the Sexy Scribblers. A group of romance writers who get together and write free stories for their fans.

Sign up for Valerie's newsletter and be the first to hear about new releases, receive special excerpts and exclusive contests. http://valerietwombly.com/newsletter-sign/

Follow Valerie
www.valerietwombly.com

THE ETERNALLY MATED SERIES

Fall into Darkness: 2nd place: THE ANCIENT CITY ROMANCE AUTHORS'
2016 HEART OF EXCELLENCE READERS' CHOICE AWARDS

&

Finalist: Heart of Denver Romance Writer's Aspen Gold Contest

Find more Valerie Twombly books at http://valerietwombly.com
Where your supernatural seduction begins

A JINN'S SEDUCTION SERIES

Spanish Nights: Winner of Best Short Fantasy, Preditors & Editors

Find more Valerie Twombly books at http://valerietwombly.com
Where your supernatural seduction begins

THE DEMONIC DESIRES SERIES

Taken by Desire : Winner of the
2016 ACRA Heart of Excellence Award
in Paranormal Romance

Find more Valerie Twombly books at
http://valerietwombly.com
Where your supernatural seduction begins

An Angel's Torment (Eternally Mated Prequel)

Veiled In Darkness (Eternally Mated #2)

Fall Into Darkness (Eternally Mated #1)

Bound By Darkness (Eternally Mated Novel)

Surrender To Darkness (Eternally Mated Novel)

Unleash The Darkness (Eternally Mated Novella)

Eternal Flame (Guardians #1)

Fatal Desire (Guardians #2)

Primal Hunger (Guardians #3)

Divine Passion (Guardians #3.5)

Amazon Heat (Demon Heat #1)

Emerald Fire (Demon Heat #2)

Spanish Nights, A Jinn's Seduction

Sultry Nights, A Jinn's Seduction

Taken By Desire (Demonic Desires #1)

His Burning Desire (Sparks Of Desire)

Passion Awakened (Beyond The Mist)

www.ingramcontent.com/pod-product-compliance
Lightning Source LLC
Chambersburg PA
CBHW031305060726
47590CB00003B/1077